MIDNIGHT AT MYSTIC INN

MYSTIC INN MYSTERIES

STEPHANIE DAMORE

ONE

"I can't believe tonight's the big night," Misty, my best friend, and owner of Spellbinding Books, said to me as she straightened her front display table. With the new year only hours away, Misty and her assistant Vicki had been busy rearranging the bookshop. Holiday displays promising a magical Christmas that would rival the North Pole had been replaced with potion cookbooks that guaranteed to slim with every spoonful and spellbooks that would make sticking to your new year's resolutions a snap. A slim blue volume with silver lettering titled *10 Simple Spells to a New You* caught my eye. I picked up the book and flipped it over to read the back.

"I bet you could teach that author a thing or two," Misty said with a smile.

"I doubt that." I may have reinvented my life not too long ago, but I was hardly an expert. I opened the book and scanned the index. The first spell was a decluttering charm followed by a glamour cream, and if all else failed, the book offered a guilt potion that would eat away at your conscience until you checked off your to-do list.

"Careful on that last one. I gave it a go over Christmas, and I wasn't able to sleep until I mailed out every Christmas card, wrapped every present, and frosted every cookie," Vicki said to me as she passed by.

I looked at the book in a new light and decided to put it back where I'd found it. If Vicki, a witch who knew what she was doing, had that strong of a reaction to the potion, who knew what I'd end up feeling guilty about? A flash of my ex-boyfriend popped into my head, specifically Allen and the elephant incident. It was a magical accident, of course, and he no longer remembered it, but that didn't mean I didn't sometimes feel guilty about how our relationship had come to an end.

Not all of my relationships had such disastrous endings. Take my former high school boyfriend, Vance Blackwell. Just thinking about how we managed to find our way back together again made me blush, which I would deny if anyone called me out on it.

"What are you thinking about?" Misty said, catching the heat rising on my cheeks.

So much for hiding my thoughts. "Nothing." I turned abruptly away and pretended to look at the new charms section.

"Uh-huh, you're thinking about Vance and what he's going to say when he sees you in that dress tonight."

I whipped back around. "I can't believe I let you talk me into buying it. It's ridiculous."

"You mean it's gorgeous. If you're not going to get glammed up tonight of all nights, when are you ever? Your wedding day?"

I balked. Yes, I loved Vance, but neither one of us was itching to race down the aisle. We headed that way once, and it ended in a spectacular disaster. I think we both had a bit of cold feet on that front, or maybe it was just me. Truthfully, neither of us had brought it up, and I was perfectly fine with that. I was still glowing with the newness of it all.

"I see I've rendered you speechless," Misty smiled, and I wanted to pummel her. Our relationship was like that, more like sisters who could nettle one another and get on each other's nerves than mere friends.

"Enough about me, what about you? You have a hot date with a rock star tonight."

It was Misty's turn to blush. She had been dating Daniel McEwan ever since he mysteriously stumbled back in town last month after his, should I say, life-altering experience. Thankfully, Daniel was back to being alive and well and 100 percent witch. With the new lease on life, Daniel said he was re-evaluating what was important to him, which meant taking risks that mattered. I wasn't sure what that meant, but perhaps it had something to do with dating Misty.

"Oh no, heads up." Vicki motioned to the two women walking into the bookstore. I didn't recognize either one of them.

"A bookstore, really? You know how I feel about reading," the dark-haired woman said to her companion.

"If you can drag me to every boutique in town, you can spend five minutes in a bookstore. It won't kill you," the other woman quipped. With her auburn hair pulled back in a messy bun and round-rimmed glasses, this woman looked nothing like her friend, who was decked out head to toe in designer labels, and what I was hoping was faux fur.

"It just might," the woman grumbled, looking around the bookstore with distaste. Her friend chose to ignore the comment and continued to browse the store as her fashionable companion trailed behind her.

I looked to Vicki with confusion in my eyes.

"You don't recognize her?" Vicki kept her voice low.

I shook my head.

"That's Rebecca from Witch News Network."

"Who?"

Misty rolled her eyes. "She's a new anchor from the East Coast. Rumor has it she was pretty ticked when they sent her here and not New York City for tonight."

Vicki nodded as my eyes widened with understanding. "She's covering the party tonight," I surmised.

Misty piped up, "And her sister, Paige, has been my best customer since they rolled into town two days ago."

I looked at the contrasting duo. Bits of their conversation floated our way. "We don't have time for this. My look needs to be flawless tonight, even if I'm not in Times Square." Rebecca continued to bemoan being in the bookstore.

"Almost done," Paige replied in a cheerful voice, which only seemed to grate on her sister's nerves.

"Hurry up!" she snapped back before sighing in dramatic fashion.

"Well, hello!" Mayor Parrish said as she strolled into the bookshop in a flutter. The mayor was dressed in a rich purple wool coat and a matching wide-brimmed hat that would befit for the Queen. Black leather gloves and plenty of gold jewelry completed the look. Mayor Parrish slid her hands out of the gloves. They were more of a fashion accessory than anything. The unseasonably warm weather was welcome on a night like tonight when everyone would be wearing formal wear and dancing the night away at Wishing Well Park. "Can you believe it's finally here?" Mayor Parrish was giddy with excitement. There was nothing she loved more than drawing attention to Silverlake, and as the mayor, tonight was her time to shine. "You should be closing soon, shouldn't you? I expect to see the three of you there tonight, looking your best. We want to show that the locals of Silverlake can shine too!" Mayor Parrish gave a nervous laugh.

"We'll be there," I spoke for our trio.

Mayor Parrish leaned forward and directed her attention to Misty.

"Now I know you're dating Daniel and all, but you need to keep your distance tonight." Mayor Parrish looked stern. "He needs to be focused and play his best. No distractions tonight, do you hear me?"

"Um, yes?" Misty hesitated, knowing arguing would be futile.

"I'm serious. After tonight's over, you can kidnap Daniel and take him to the Maldives for all I care. But for tonight, the entertainment needs to be perfect. Tonight is going to be magical. I can feel it. Oh!" Mayor Parrish caught sight of Rebecca and her sister. "I see someone I need to talk to." Mayor Parrish held her hand to the side of her mouth as if imparting a secret but didn't bother lowering her voice. "Rebecca's interviewing me tonight on live television, twice! Better see what I need to prepare for." Mayor Parrish fluttered her gloves in the air as a wave and set off to talk to Rebecca.

She didn't get too far. The sisters were making their way up the aisle when they ran right into Mayor Parrish.

Misty, Vicki, and I watched the scene with unbridled curiosity.

"I'm thrilled that I bumped into you. I can't wait for the interview tonight. Now, tell me, what type of questions would you like to know? A good witch is always prepared." Mayor Parish laughed nervously again.

"I'm sorry, who are you?" Rebecca looked down her nose at Mayor Parrish.

Mayor Parrish didn't miss a beat. "Patricia

Parrish, the mayor of this beautiful town." Mayor Parrish swept her arm out in front as if showcasing the beauties of Silverlake.

"Listen, I don't mean to be rude, but I don't care—"

"What my sister means to say is that she can't wait for tonight and your interview, but we really must be going," Paige jumped in before Rebecca could insult Mayor Parrish any further. "If you'd like, I can check with the producer and see what questions he's prepared. If you give me your number, I'll give you a call as soon as I have them. Does that work?"

"Well, yes, I suppose that does. How very thoughtful of you." Mayor Parrish dug around in her handbag for a moment before retrieving a business card from its gold case. "Here's my number. I can't wait for tonight," Mayor Parrish directed the last statement to Rebecca, who had shifted her attention out the window and ignored the mayor.

"All set?" Misty stepped forward, seeing a book in Paige's hand.

Paige looked relieved for the interruption and readily followed Misty to the checkout counter. Rebecca continued to stare out the window. It was only then that I realized her gaze hadn't been mindless. She was watching someone. The question was who. Plenty of people milled about, getting last-minute goodies for New Year's Eve parties or purchasing accessories for tonight's grand affair, but Rebecca looked transfixed.

"First time to Silverlake?" I interrupted her thoughts. Rebecca snapped her attention to me. "I was just wondering if you saw someone out there that you knew."

Rebecca opened and closed her mouth like a fish out of water. I smiled in return. I couldn't help myself after the way Rebecca had treated Mayor Parrish. Mayor Parrish might be a pain in the butt, but she was our pain in the butt. Like it or not, us locals stuck together.

"No, no one." Rebecca snapped her mouth shut. "You about ready?" She hollered over to her sister before adding under her breath, "The sooner I can get out of here, the better."

After Misty finished ringing up Paige, I left with a promise to meet my friend at center stage at eight o'clock. Seeing I hadn't driven into town, I started the short walk back to the inn. It would've been quicker to hop on the Enchanted Trail, the footpath that skirted the perimeter of the lake, but even I had to admit I was excited for tonight. I couldn't resist walking past Wishing Well Park and taking one last peek at the preparations for the big event. As I strolled across the parking lot toward Wishing Well Park, my eyes scrolled up, up, and up some more until they focused on the giant ball suspended above a specially designed platform. The ball was easily ten feet in diameter, maybe even more. I squinted as I looked up, trying to make out the details. The outside appeared to be covered in mirrors and lights, the reflective coating catching the late afternoon rays of sunshine.

"What do you think? Will it work?" the man's voice said from beside me. I hadn't even realized Mr. McCormick had joined me.

"I think it looks great. It's the countdown ball, right?"

"Yep, it has over a thousand lights, but Mayor Parrish doesn't think it's bright enough. She asked what else I could come up with."

"What more does she want?"

"Bigger, brighter, just more, I guess." Mr. McCormick shrugged. "I'm not quite sure what I'll do yet."

"Anything I can do to help?" Engorgement charms weren't my thing unless you wanted to turn someone into an elephant. Even then, I couldn't promise it would work.

"Nah, it'll be all right. And if not, no one will know the difference." I had to admire Mr. McCormick's laid-back attitude. If I had been in charge of tonight's ball drop, I'd be a nervous wreck. Just thinking about being responsible for a high-profile event on live television was enough to make my eye twitch. It was amazing that I had pulled off so many large-scale events in my previous life in Chicago. Then again, that probably explained why I had been wound up so tight before coming back home. Time and time again, the universe reminded me why being back in Silverlake was good for me.

"If you think of anything I can help with, give the inn a call. Aunt Thelma and I will be there getting ready."

"You got it, but I have an idea. Let me see if this works first." Mr. McCormick didn't elaborate any further, and I didn't ask.

"Good luck. I'll see you tonight."

TWO

In the distance, workers brought in from WNN continued setting up for the event. An elaborate stage stood front and center. This was nothing like the grandstand Mr. McCormick had built in the fall. No, this was a professional setup for Daniel's band. Overhead concert lights, large speakers, and a black backdrop with the band's logo dominated the space. A wooden dance floor covered half of the park's lawn. Bare-bulb lights surrounded the perimeter and criss-crossed the floor above. The network had even thought to bring in propane heaters if the air turned chilly. However, rumor had it that Connie, down at the potions shop, was providing magical hot choco-late that warmed you from the inside out, and who could forget the fire whiskey our local tavern was famous for. We were sure to be warm and toasty tonight.

I looked down at my phone. Perhaps Rebecca had been right to be worried about the time. Late afternoon was quickly slipping away to early evening, and I also needed to start getting ready. Speaking of which, I thought I should give Vance a call and make sure our plans hadn't changed. Being the premier defense attorney in our magical community meant you never knew when some bizarre case would drop on your lap. It was often at the most inconvenient time.

"Hey, I was just thinking about you," Vance said when he answered.

"Well, that's always nice to hear. How's it going with you?"

"Good. Well, mostly good."

"Oh no, I don't like the sound of that."

"It's nothing too bad. Terry and Tommy Robertson were arrested again today."

"Are you serious? What did they do now?" The Robertson brothers were always getting into trouble. If a town could have resident juvenile delinquents, they were it.

"Stole Mrs. Potts' car."

"What? They did not. Do they even have their license? Is the car okay?"

"The oldest, Terry, has his license. The car is fine, and it's back in Mrs. Potts' driveway. The boys claim they asked her to borrow it, and she doesn't remember. She says they're full of it."

"My money's on Mrs. Potts. She might be getting old, but her memory's as sharp as ever."

"I agree. The best thing I can probably do is get them community service this time."

"And talk to their parents. They can't keep covering for these boys forever."

"Have you ever talked to the Robertsons?"

"I see your point." Mrs. Robertson was the type of mom who believed her children could do no wrong. "Do you still want to pick me up tonight, or should we meet up at the park?"

"I will be picking you up. I've been looking forward to it all day."

"Me too." I smiled on my end of the phone. "I'll let you go then. I'm walking back to the inn right now to start getting ready."

"You be careful. You have your wand?"

"Do I have my wand," I replied sarcastically.

Vance was silent on his end of the line, waiting for me to confirm.

I cleared my throat and fessed up. "Actually, I think I left it at home. But!" I interjected before Vance could lecture me. "It's only because I was in a hurry to run into town, and I promise you I've been carrying it every day." Almost every day. There were some habits that were harder than others to get into. "Anyway, I can see the inn from here." Or I would be able to see the inn as soon as I rounded the next bend. "I'll see you at seven-thirty?"

"It's a date."

"Okay, I love you. See you soon."

"I love you too." Vance practically sighed into the phone. I tried not to smile at his exasperation. I had to hand it to my boyfriend. He was a trooper. He never gave me grief for following my crazy instincts wherever they led me, which was usually into trouble, but even I knew it was reckless to walk around wandless. The downfall to Silverlake becoming popular meant that more strangers were coming through town regularly. Tonight was no exception. Witches from around the region had flocked to Silverlake for the WNN party. Vance was right. I needed to carry my wand on me at all times. A mistake I wouldn't make again in the future.

When I got back to the inn, there was a line at the check-in counter five deep. I quickly tugged off my coat and threw it in the back office before joining my aunt on the other side of the counter.

"Why didn't you call me?" I said in a rush as I took over for Percy, the poltergeist, so that he could help with guests' luggage.

"Oh, it's nothing we can't handle," my aunt said with a smile plastered on her face.

"Speak for yourself," Percy grumbled under his breath. For the longest time, Percy and Aunt Thelma ran the inn, just the two of them year after year, which suited Percy just fine, except the inn had very few guests along with the rest of Silver-lake. The once quaint village was rapidly turning into a ghost town. Great if you're a ghost. Not so great if you owned an inn and were trying to make a living.

"Hello, welcome to Mystic Inn. Do you have a reservation?" Aunt Thelma asked the silver-haired gentleman before her.

"Isn't this nice. I haven't been here for years. It looks like you've done a bit of work." The gentleman looked around the lobby with appreciation. While his gaze was diverted, my aunt took a moment to fluff her hair and make sure her necklace dangled on her décolletage just so. I did a double-take at my aunt. What was the woman up to?

"Are you okay?" I asked under my breath as I

bent down to fetch a room key for the guest before me.

Aunt Thelma peered down at me. "Just fine, dear." My aunt turned her attention back to the gentleman before her. "It looks like you'll be staying here through the weekend?"

"That's the plan if I can manage to avoid work for that long, but something tells me, it's not going to be as hard as I initially thought." The gentleman winked at my aunt.

I expected her to reply with some dry retort, but instead, I was stunned to hear her say, "No, I don't expect it will be."

As soon as the gentleman walked away, my aunt returned back to her normal self.

"Do you know him?"

"Not now," My aunt patted my hand and turned to greet the next guest in line.

Speaking of which, the line seemed to be never-ending. The minute the last guest approached the desk, two more queued behind him.

"I didn't think we were full tonight," I said in the seconds between wishing the last guest a pleasant stay and welcoming a new one.

"I think tonight's excitement was too much to ignore," my aunt remarked.

I looked up and eyed the line and noticed Paige

had joined the end of it. Paige and her sister were already checked in, which meant she needed something for her current room. "Percy, do you mind finishing checking in the Collins for me?" I said to the poltergeist as I sidestepped around the counter to meet Paige and see what I could do to help.

The young woman looked sheepish. "I know it's probably a long shot, and I feel bad for even asking, but my sister's wondering if you have a room that's a bit more grand." Paige paused before saying the last word.

I blinked. "Grand? You mean besides the lakefront suite? That's pretty much as grand as it gets here in Silverlake." At least as far as I knew. There was a bed-and-breakfast in town that had a handful of rooms, but I couldn't imagine they'd be anything glamorous. Silverlake's style tended to run on the charming side versus high-end.

"That's what I thought. And I do love the sliding glass door and being able to step out and see the lake. But you know Rebecca. She was hoping for a hot tub and walk-in closet, maybe some chocolate-covered strawberries and champagne." In other words, a luxury resort.

"We have champagne. I can send that up, and I'm pretty sure I have strawberries, but not chocolate-dipped ones." Aunt Thelma kept the wine and champagne stocked for guests, and we offered fresh fruit and pastries for guests every morning, but not chocolate-covered ones. That would require a special trip to Luke at The Candy Cauldron. Diane sometimes had them at the bakery, but since she and Roger eloped on Christmas day, I wasn't counting on it. "And your room has a soaking tub, but that's about the best I can do there." Aunt Thelma and I had talked about adding a hot tub to the deck outside, and it was still something we planned to do, but not until spring. With the lake out front, we never had a reason for a pool, and all of my hotel connections told me that en suite whirlpools were more hassle than they were worth. A witch could always drop in a bath charm or two to customize their bath experience, which is why I found myself offering to run into town and do the same for Rebecca. "I can probably grab a magical bath bomb or two. What does your sister like? Vanilla, lavender, eucalyptus oil? A few of the shops in Village Square carry them." My favorite was the rose oil infinity bomb. Not only did it turn your bath water pink and leave your skin amazingly soft, but the little ball of wonder emitted bubbles for a solid thirty minutes. What more could a witch want?

"You know what, I can't believe I didn't think to do that. That's a great idea. I'll head back into town."

"Are you sure? I could send our concierge. I'm sure he wouldn't mind.

Percy glared at me from behind the registration desk. The ghost served as our concierge, valet, and all-around handyman. Passing away as an old man had left him with plenty of life experience and a mischievous personality, which was probably why he was grumpy, having to work so hard today. The child in him was ready to go out and play. I'd have to be on my toes for the next few days waiting for him to retaliate. Hopefully, he couldn't find a toad anywhere in January.

"No, that's okay. It's my job, after all. With Rebecca getting ready for tonight's show, she'll be in the bathroom for at least the next two hours. She probably won't even notice I'm gone." Paige replied with a self-deprecating smile.

I hoped my expression didn't show how much I pitied her. I didn't envy Paige one bit. Working for Rebecca would be a nightmare. "If you change your mind, just give a call down to the front desk."

Paige thanked me again and disappeared back down the hall.

Thirty minutes later, Aunt Thelma and I had finally managed to clear out the lobby.

"Are you sure you're going to be able to manage all this when I'm gone?"

As soon as the words were past my lips, I regretted them instantly. Of course, Aunt Thelma could handle the inn by herself for four days. She had managed Mystic Inn for more than a decade when I lived in Chicago. It's not like she would run the place into the ground in four days. At least, I hoped she wouldn't. Still, it would be a lot of work with a full house.

"You know I can. Plus, I have plenty of help around here. Hiring the extra weekend help was a brilliant idea. You and Vance go and have fun. Don't you dare think about using me as an excuse to cancel your vacation."

"I swear, that's not what I'm doing. I'm quite looking forward to our getaway." I leaned closer into the mirror to apply my lipstick. I hadn't planned on going all out, but once Misty had talked me into the dress and Aunt Thelma had persuaded me to buy the shoes, there was no other way to complete the look.

Aunt Thelma was doing the same, primping in front of the mirror. Only her cosmetic of choice was her wand. A little zap here, a tightening there, and my aunt was glammed up and good to go.

"Here, look at me."

I stood and looked over my shoulder, and the moment I did, my aunt blasted me with a beauty spell right to the face. I didn't even have a moment to object.

"There, now you're ready for tonight. Shall we?" Again, my aunt didn't wait for a reply as she swept out of the hall bathroom.

I silently shook my head and trailed after.

Aunt Thelma and I busied ourselves putting on the final touches. I'd purchased a faux fur wrap to go with my long-sleeved, black lace dress in case the air turned crisp. I needed something to keep me warm. My dress was short, and the material form-fitting. To say it was a different look for me was an understatement. I had attended plenty of formal events in Chicago, but it was always as an event coordinator wearing a simple black dress to help me blend in with the crowd and make sure everything was running smoothly. The only thing about me that was the same was the tiger eye pendant resting against my chest. I never took the necklace off. It was a family heirloom, but more than that, it gave me, and only me, the power to transform into a cat. I'd excelled in transformation spells in my youth, but now days it was hit or miss. Just look to the butterfly paperclips floating around the inn as an example. The paperclips never did fully transform into butter-flies, and they were lightning fast, making them impossible to catch.

A moment later, there was a knock on the door. The sound snapped me out of my thoughts. "Oh, that's probably Vance. I'll get it." I slipped on my black heels and made my way to the door, but the moment I opened it, I was shocked to find the silver-haired gentleman from this afternoon on the other side.

"Frederick, so good to see you again. Come on in. I'm just fetching my coat." Aunt Thelma shot me a secret smile before disappearing into the front coat closet.

My brain was still whirling with the unexpected turn of events, and it took me a minute to find my manners. Apparently, I was the only one.

"Frederick Kringle, nice to meet you." The gentleman extended his hand.

"Angelica Nightingale. Pleased to meet you. Come on in." I stood back from the door to allow the gentleman to walk inside. "Can I get you to anything before I head out?" When in doubt, I could always be trusted to fall back into hospitality mode.

"No, it's okay, dear. We're leaving right behind you."

"Knock, knock," Vance said as he rapped on the door with a single knuckle. "Wow, you look stunning." Vance only had eyes for me.

"You're welcome," Aunt Thelma said over her

shoulder as she tossed a sheer scarf around her neck. I shot my aunt a look. "Not that you're not beautiful on your own," Aunt Thelma bristled. "What do you say, Frederick? Shall we be off?" My aunt changed the subject.

Vance registered my aunt's date for the first time. Frederick replied to Vance's acknowledgment with a head nod.

"I guess we shall." Frederick held out his elbow, which my aunt readily accepted, and the two quickly left into the evening.

"Who's that?" Vance asked, leaning back to see the two make their exit.

"A guest. His name's Frederick Kringle, and that's all I know, but I expect we will be hearing more about him in the future."

"Knowing your aunt, I'm sure we will."

THREE

Silverlake was on full display. As a local, I couldn't be prouder, and you couldn't ask for more as the inn's manager. Waitstaff weaved their way through the crowd. I eyed the tray as it passed by, noting Luke's chocolate truffles, Diane's petit fours, and appetizers from the Simmering Spoon. Connie was there too, trailing behind, passing out her magical hot chocolate to keep everyone feeling nice and toasty. The positive energy in the air filled me with excitement. Mayor Parrish was right. Tonight was going to be magical.

"Champagne?" Vance asked me. In the back of the park was a white tent filled with tables and chairs, and from the looks of it, a complete bar.

"That would be great, thanks." Vance excused himself and made his way through the crowd. Vicki spotted me and gave me a wave, as did my aunt's best friend, Clemmie. I continued to scan the group to see who else I recognized. Rebecca was front and center, standing under the giant ball on a dais, interviewing Daniel.

"Oh, excuse me. Sorry about that." Luke did a double-take. "Angelica?"

"Don't look so surprised," I teased, but even I knew I didn't look like myself.

"You look stunning. Sorry for running right into you." Luke looked back up to the stage. It looked like someone else had caught the chocolatier's eye tonight.

"Do you think she's single?" Luke's eyes never left the stage.

"Rebecca? You don't want to date Rebecca. Trust me, she's staying at the inn, and she's something else."

"Not the news anchor. The girl off to the side." Luke motioned to the left of the stage. "I've never seen her before. Do you know who she is?" I had to crane my neck to see who Luke was referring to. "Oh, you mean Paige. She's Rebecca's sister, and she is a sweetheart. You have my full blessing there."

"Think you could introduce us?"

"I'd be happy to. Let me just text Vance that we'll be up by the stage. He ran off to get drinks." Luke waited while I did just that, and then the two of us weaved our way through the crowd. I had to admit, there were more people at this party that I didn't know than I did. I guess I shouldn't be surprised that the inn was booked after all.

"Is your sister here?" I had yet to see Sally or her troublemaking twin daughters, Beatrice and Sabrina.

"Ha, no. My sister took them to Disney World. With a night like tonight, she figured she better play it safe and get the girls out of town."

I looked at Vance like I wasn't following.

"You think my nieces could resist doing something crazy on live TV?"

"Good point. Your sister's a smart one."

"Yeah, she got all the brains in the family." Luke smiled when he said it, so I knew he was joking.

Paige stood off to the side of the stage, looking like her sister's personal coat rack. She had two bags and a coat hanging from each arm. Her expression was distant, and she looked like she was having anything but fun.

"Here, let me help you with those." Luke didn't wait for Paige to reply before taking the bags from her hands.

"Oh, you don't have to do that. I'll be holding these all night."

"Paige, this is my friend Luke. He owns The Candy Cauldron in town," I explained.

"The one that makes those delicious truffles? They're amazing. If my sister weren't so obsessed with her figure, I would have bought a dozen."

Luke and Paige continued to talk, the conversation switching from chocolate to things to do around Silverlake. I excused myself to go find Vance and found Misty two steps later. "Hey, good-looking, what's cooking." She bumped her hip into mine. "I told you you'd look amazing in that dress."

"Why, thank you. You look pretty hot yourself." Misty had gone for the rockstar look, and she had pulled it off flawlessly. Not everyone could make black leather pants look good.

Misty didn't respond. She was too busy locking eyes with Daniel.

"Hello, Earth to Misty," I waved my hand in front of her face.

Misty dodged my hand and never broke eye contact.

"Oh my gosh, you're in love."

That snapped her out of it. Misty swatted my arm. "I am not in love. I am Misty Mayweather McQuade. I do not fall in love with gorgeous rockstars."

"Okay, fine. You're infatuated with him, then—a total fangirl. Better go line up by the tour bus," I laughed at Misty's horrified expression.

"No, I was infatuated with him in high school, if you must know."

"And let's face it, who wasn't? Well, besides me."

"That's only because you had Vance."

"This is true."

"What are we talking about?" Vance asked, joining the party with two glasses of champagne. He handed me one of the glass flutes.

"Just that Misty is in love with Daniel." I took a sip of champagne and looked up innocently.

"I am not in love!" Misty's eyes went wide, and I could tell she was itching to stomp her foot. She probably would've if her heel wouldn't have sunk straight into the ground. Not to mention Daniel was done with his interview and was heading our way. Misty excused herself and went to meet him halfway. If I knew Misty, she wasn't taking any chances. She'd rather turn tail and run than risk us bringing up the L Word in Daniel's presence. Not that I would. That was something she would do if the roles were reversed. In fact, before Vance and I rekindled our relationship, Misty had no problem dropping Vance and love in the same sentence. And like my relationship with Vance, I could tell Misty cared for Daniel. I'd known her long enough to see that plain as day. Just like I knew it terrified her to death. Again, I could relate. I only hoped Misty could be honest with herself sooner rather than later.

Rebecca quickly recaptured my attention.

"Where have you been!" The news anchor demanded as she stepped off the circular stage and stomped over to Paige. "I'm freezing. Give me my coat."

Paige looked abashed by her sister's behavior as Rebecca snatched the coat off her arm. "Where are the rest of my bags?"

Vance and I exchanged a look. I couldn't believe how rude Rebecca was.

"Right here," Luke extended his arm, "I was giving your sister a hand."

"Which, I told him it wasn't necessary, but he insisted." Paige looked up at Luke with a smile.

"Of course, it's not necessary. It's your job." Rebecca rolled her eyes. Then she held out her hand. "Lip gloss."

Paige broke eye contact with Luke and began rummaging around in one of Rebecca's bags, quickly retrieving a tube of shiny pink gloss.

Rebecca swiped at her top and bottom lip like a pro before handing it back to her sister without even looking. "Now, where's Cameron? I need to remind him to stop shooting me from the right. I swear if he doesn't listen, I'm going to have to throttle him." I had no doubt that Rebecca meant every word.

"You, stay." Rebecca talked to Paige as if she were a dog in obedience training.

Again, Paige didn't even bother to reply.

"She's something else, isn't she?" The middle-aged woman said from beside Vance. Unlike the rest of us, the woman hadn't dressed in formal wear. She wore brown leather boots, black leggings, and a patchwork coat. At that moment, I wished we could switch wardrobes, as she looked much more comfortable than I did. I had only been wearing my high heels for an hour, and the arches of my feet were already starting to cramp.

"That she is," I remarked as I watched Rebecca beeline it for the cameraman and light into him. I'd met Cameron briefly at the inn. We didn't chat much. Last night he sat in the lobby for a portion of the evening, checking his equipment, and I didn't dare interrupt.

The woman beside me shook her head, and I couldn't tell if it was in distaste or admiration. It was sort of like watching a train wreck. You knew you shouldn't stare, but yet you couldn't look away.

Just then, Clemmie sashayed past, and I had to say hello.

"Wow, Clemmie. I love the look."

Like my aunt, Clemmie rarely looked her age, which, you guessed it, was due more to potions and spells than good genes.

"This old thing?" Clemmie chuckled. She was rocking a 1920s theme with a flapper dress and feathered headband. Clemmie led the town's retired attorney, Boyd Andrews, out to the dance floor. The portly gentleman could barely keep up, but that didn't stop him from trying. Since retiring, Boyd seemed to be living his best life. Every time I ran into him, he talked about playing bingo at the senior center or taking the Fortune Bus north to the casino in North Carolina. I never thought to pair Clemmie and Boyd together, but now that I saw them laughing and dancing, I wondered why it had never occurred to me before.

A couple of hours later, we found a slice of solitude when Daniel's band slowed it down, and Vance asked me to dance. The night was clear, the stars were bright, and even though hundreds of people surrounded us, the moment felt perfect. Or it would've if I hadn't spotted Rebecca berating Cameron again. Unfortunately, we were close enough to hear parts of the conversation.

"Do I have to be in the same frame as the blue-berry? She's ruining my airtime." It didn't take much to figure out who Rebecca was talking about. One look at Mayor Parrish in her deep blue velvet gown, waiting in the wings to be interviewed, gave it away. For the second time that day, Rebecca had insulted the poor woman. Thankfully, the mayor hadn't heard her, or the comment would've crushed her. Mayor Parrish was beaming, looking over the crowd and waiting for her time in front of the camera.

Cameron looked up at the mayor and back down to Rebecca. You could see the wheels inside of his head turning. "I wouldn't say that,"he said hesitantly.

"What do you mean? Look at her! Gross."

"It's just, ah, think of it this way. Being next to her makes you look better." Cameron looked unsure even as he said the words. It was like trying to placate a toddler. You never knew if your strategy was going to backfire or not.

"Oh my gosh, you're right. Why didn't I think of that? I love it! You're so smart. That's why I adore you. I do." Rebecca talked in a baby voice, leaned forward, and pinched the cameraman's cheeks.

Cameron swallowed uncomfortably.

"You know what?" Rebecca didn't wait for Cameron to respond. "Maybe we should add in another interview. You know she won't say no to being on camera." Rebecca snickered at the mayor's expense.

"Sure, if that's what you want to do." Cameron put the ball back in Rebecca's court, which was probably the smartest thing for him to do.

Rebecca clapped her hands in excitement.

"Let's do it. You're the best!"

"Er, I do what I can." Cameron stumbled over his words.

"I really don't like her," I confessed to Vance.

He looked over my shoulder and knew exactly who I was talking about. "It's amazing how much she changes when the cameras are on."

"Alarming is more like it. Who would've thought someone could be so two-faced? I can't imagine being that way."

Vance leaned low so that his cheek was pressed to mine. "That's because you're a good person." Vance twirled me away from Rebecca and her drama.

I smiled up at him. "So are you." I leaned forward, rested my cheek on his shoulder, and closed my eyes, shutting out the rest of the world and letting the music and the moment float me away.

It was finally almost midnight. I had kicked off my heels long ago. They lay discarded underneath one of the many pecan trees that dotted the property. I crossed my fingers that I would remember which tree it was tomorrow. If not, it would be good practice for a summoning charm. I was getting pretty good at them, given how often Aunt Thelma misplaced her wand or lost her car keys, but sometimes my magic still went awry. Like last week when I was looking for her keys and I somehow summoned Carol Keyes, the retired librarian in town. The poor woman was hard of hearing, and she couldn't understand why she felt compelled to drive to the inn. I tried fruitlessly to explain the error, but I'm not sure she ever got it. In the end, Aunt Thelma gave her a pastry from the morning buffet and sent the sweet lady on her way. Percy was still giving me grief about it.

As the seconds ticked closer to midnight, the crowd gathered around the center stage to watch the ball drop. I caught Mr. McCormick's eye as he stood in the front, making sure the crowd backed up a bit. When our eyes met, he gave me a thumbs up, which I took as a good sign that all was well with whatever he had planned.

Finally, with less than a minute to go, the bright colors on the ball began to light up in a dizzying array. First, a wave of blue lights circled the ball, followed by a wave of purple and then gold. The crowd oohed and ahhed at the light display. More than a few raised their champagne glasses, preparing to toast to the new year.

"We should do this every year," Aunt Thelma said with excitement in her voice.

"Mmm-hmm. If you like this sort of thing." But even Clemmie couldn't hide the smile from her face.

I looked behind my aunt and to her other side. "Where's Frederick?"

My aunt waived my question away. "Threw his back out doing the Electric Slide. Don't worry, I already called Constantine, and Frederick insisted I come back out. I wasn't about to argue with the man. You know how I love a good party." Constantine was our town healer. She was like a traditional medical doctor, only one who specialized in magical remedies. Frederick was in good hands.

The crowd began to chant the countdown, "Ten! Nine! Eight!" The ball slowly started to descend. Rebecca stood off to the side, microphone in hand, talking excitedly into the camera. Her eyes sparkled, and her smile appeared genuine. Like there was nowhere else in the world she'd rather be. Rebecca's words were drowned out by the crowd. Once again, I was reminded what a different person she was when the camera was rolling. She couldn't leave Silverlake soon enough.

Vance stood beside me and squeezed my hand. I looked up at him and smiled. Like the rest of the crowd, I couldn't wait to shout Happy New Year momentarily.

In the next second, gold fountains erupted on the ground from the base of the stage. People cheered with delight as the fireworks accented the light display. I finally understood why Mr. McCormick kept insisting everyone back up. He was trying to keep everyone safe.

"Three! Two! One!"

The second the ball hit the base, a blinding blue light shot out. The force was so strong that it knocked the wind out of my lungs and stole the celebratory shouts from my lips. An icy blast blew through the crowd and rippled across the lake like a sonic boom. A few people had been knocked backward by the force.

In an instant, the park's fountain froze, and thick snowflakes began to fall.

Every molecule of heat had been zapped away from my body, leaving me chilled to the bone. I wasn't the only one. Around us, partygoers helped one another to their feet and huddled together as they took in the cursed winter wonderland that had descended on our magical evening.

"What in the world just happened?" Clemmie rubbed her exposed shoulders to try to generate some heat.

I spotted the woman from before, the one wearing the comfortable clothes, laughing. It was an odd reaction given the turn of events.

"You all right?" Vance said, turning to me and giving me a once-over with his eyes. I was too stunned to speak. I found myself nodding in response. I was about to ask him the same when a gasp rippled through the air, followed by eerie silence.

"Oh my," Aunt Thelma exclaimed, catching a peek of the scene before us.

"Well, isn't that something?" Clemmie added in wonder.

"What, what is it?" I should have kept my heels on. I had no hope of seeing over the crowd.

Moments later, people began to part in shock, and I saw the reason for the commotion.

It was Rebecca and Mayor Parrish. They were standing on the middle of the stage, and they were frozen solid.

FOUR

A lot seemed to happen in the immediate aftermath. The temperature had plummeted, turning the mild night into a frigid Arctic winter. Vance took off his sportscoat and covered me with it.

"No, I'm fine," I said, trying to hand it back through chattering teeth. My toes were quickly growing numb, as were my fingertips. We all needed to get inside soon. The propane heaters were no match for the winter storm that had now settled upon Silverlake.

Connie had conjured up as much magical hot chocolate as possible and was passing out the cups to everyone. "Hot chocolate?" Connie said from behind us. I turned around and readily accepted the drink from the potion master's outstretched hand. One of her coworkers held a tray, and Connie handed out the warm beverages as quickly as she could. After a few sips, the magical brew started to thaw my insides, but I was still cold.

"I've got fire whiskey at the tavern. If you want some, it's on the house," Bonnie Daniels hollered over the crowd. Bonnie and her husband Craig owned the tavern on the other side of the parking lot in Village Square. "Craig's stoking the fire right now. Come on in, and we'll get you warmed up real quick." Bonnie gave a sweeping motion with her arm before turning around and walking toward the tavern. Bonnie continued to extend the invitation as she walked, promising fire whiskey and a warm meal to everyone who followed her.

"That's all fine and dandy, but what in the heck just happened?" Clemmie looked around the park, which was quickly emptying.

"Did you see that light? Did anyone else see the light?" Luke asked, joining us. We all nodded that we had between shivering. "Good, because for a minute there, I thought I was the only one. What just happened?"

"That's what I'm saying." Clemmie agreed.

"I think it must be a curse." Aunt Thelma spoke softly.

"A curse?" I looked around the park, suddenly feeling very exposed out in the open.

"How else would you explain it?" Aunt Thelma seemed genuinely interested in my answer.

"I don't know, a spell gone awry?" I searched the crowd for Mr. McCormick.

"Don't look at me," the man in question stepped over to us.

"This wasn't part of your big surprise?" I asked hopefully.

"Some surprise," Clemmie grumbled.

"No, ma'am, I added the fireworks. I just told the sheriff the same thing. Speaking of which," Mr. McCormick motioned to the sheriff and his daughter heading our way.

"Which one of you thought this would be some kind of joke?" Deputy Amber Reynolds had ditched the county-commissioned, brown uniform for a pink princess gown that made her look like Barbie personified.

It didn't matter how beautiful the woman was. Her attitude still stunk.

"Now, sweetie, don't forget the camera is still rolling," her father, the sheriff, said. Unlike his daughter, Sheriff Reynolds was still in uniform. He hadn't taken the night off.

The sheriff stepped forward and pulled his

daughter to the side and then motioned to Cameron, who was still filming the entire scene. He had the camera pointed right at the duo. From the shocked expression on Cameron's face, he also seemed to forget it. Cameron looked away from the eyepiece for a moment but didn't lower the camera. Instead, he repositioned himself and scanned the scene. I thought that was a smart move. If we were going to figure out what happened, we would need all the evidence we could garner.

"What do you think we should do?" I felt weird abandoning Mayor Parrish, but we couldn't stand out here and freeze to death. Plus, we needed to get back to the inn.

"I know what I'm going to do. We need to fight magic with magic." Aunt Thelma withdrew her wand and pointed it at my chest. I ducked to the side and hid behind Vance. Freezing or not, I wasn't going to go first with one of my aunt's spells.

"Coward," my aunt pointed the wand at Vance and mumbled an incantation. The tip of her wand immitted a soft orange glow, but it was quickly snuffed out like a candle flame in the wind.

"That's not going to work. You need to think bigger. What we need is a sunlight spell. Blast this snow right out of here. I'll have it feeling balmy in no time." Clemmie bent low and lifted up the hem of her dress to retrieve her wand. My jaw about dropped. "What, you don't own a wand holster?"

"Um, no." I didn't even know they made such things.

"Now I know what you get you for your birthday," Clemmie smiled. "What do you think, Diafotízo on three?"

Aunt Thelma shrugged her shoulder in agreement. "Who knows, it's worth a shot." My aunt held her wand at the ready.

Clemmie cleared her throat and held her wand high, mirroring my aunt's pose, ready to cast the spell.

"Wait!" It took my brain a second to catch up. "You can't do that. What if you melt them?" I motioned to Mayor Parrish and Rebecca. "If you warm it up, they could melt." Unlike glacio, the spell that freezes a person in place, Mayor Parrish and Rebecca looked like ice sculptures. They were clear sparkling ice.

"She's got a point," Mr. McCormick agreed.

"I agree. It's too dangerous," Vance remarked.

Clemmie huffed, admitting defeat.

"What about my freezer?" Luke offered up. In front of us, Paige and Cameron were talking to Sheriff Reynolds. Paige kept shaking her head as if she didn't know the answer to the sheriff's questions. Then they both nodded and began to follow him, presumably for questioning. My friend, Deputy Jones, took over guarding Rebecca and Mayor Parrish.

"That's not a bad idea," Aunt Thelma said. I turned my attention back to the matter at hand. "What was that?" I hadn't picked up on Luke's comment, but I realized he must've asked something as everyone was looking to me for my opinion.

"I said, what if we keep Rebecca and Mayor Parrish in my freezer? That way, we can work on thawing Silverlake but keep them safe until we figure out how to turn them back."

"That's not a bad idea." We had a kitchen at the inn with the freezer, but it was just a small one attached to the fridge—nothing like Luke's.

"If you don't have room, I could ask my mom. She has one at the diner." Vance's mom, Heather, owned the small diner in Village Square. She served the best peach iced tea and Montecristo sandwich I've ever tasted, which was why she wasn't at the party tonight. She knew people would be hungry afterward, so she had kept the diner open late on a night when they'd usually close early.

"Hey, Deputy Jones," I said, jogging over to him. We were going to have to make this quick. Connie's magical hot chocolate was wearing off, and my toes were starting to go numb.

"Oh no, I don't like the looks of this," Deputy Jones said as our group trailed behind me.

"What's going to happen to the mayor right now? Do you know what the sheriff's thinking?" I asked.

"As a matter of fact, he said something about the morgue."

"The morgue! You can't put Mayor Parrish in the morgue. She's not dead. She's just frozen. What if he chips her putting her in that little rectangular hole or pinches her foot in the door. You think it's just a little crack, and then CRASH! Her whole foot falls off. The mayor isn't going to like that after we thaw her out and she finds out about it."

"No, I don't imagine she will, but to be honest, I have to agree with the sheriff. Where else are we going to keep them frozen and safe?" Deputy Jones looked at the two ice sculptures. I did the same. Up close, the detail was incredible. Every inch of the mayor was clear ice, right down to the buttons on her coat and the gold watch on her wrist.

I motioned to Luke with my thumb. "Luke offered up his freezer at The Candy Cauldron. I don't know about you, but if I had to be put on ice, I'd rather have it be at a candy shop than the morgue."

"You sure you have room?" Deputy Jones asked Luke.

"Positive. I cleared almost everything out, bringing it here for tonight."

"Then let me radio the sheriff and see if we can arrange that."

A couple of hours later, Vance and I were sitting in the inn's lobby, taking a moment to relax. We had been busy nonstop from the moment we got back. Some people, freaked out by the winter snowstorm, immediately checked out and headed out of town before things worsened. I knew it was bad when guests weren't even asking for refunds. They just wanted to get the heck out of town. Other people made the trip over from the campground and were looking for a warm bed after their campsites became buried in snow. I didn't blame them. While I enjoyed camping, I didn't like the thought of sleeping in a tent with snow falling outside.

But now, things had quieted down. Vance had helped me set out extra blankets for guests, and Aunt Thelma had whipped up a hot chocolate bar complete with candy canes, chocolate sprinkles, and mini marshmallows to try to make the situation as cozy as possible. A fire roared in the lobby's hearth too. The scene was right out of a Christmas movie, except for the fact that Christmas had passed and we'd never experienced a cursed blizzard before, which was what I was starting to think of it as.

"You should go to bed. I'll keep an eye on things." Vance stood behind the registration desk, his arms resting on the countertop. Percy had dashed out into the snow the minute the line had died down, and the poltergeist had yet to return. At least someone was happy with the change of events.

"Thanks, I appreciate it, but I can't sleep." I was either too worked up, or maybe I was overtired at that point. It was hard to tell the difference.

The lobby's front door opened momentarily, and Paige slipped through and pulled the door shut behind her before the force of the wind could blow it all the way open. Once safely inside, Paige stood in the foyer for a moment, looking lost.

"Glad you made it back." I stepped over to the door and directed Paige to sit by the fire.

"Yes, that nice Deputy Jones gave me a lift. I was worried I was going to have to spend the night at the sheriff's department."

"I'm sorry. I should've given you my number. Vance has a truck. We could have come and got you."

"No, it's all right. You didn't know this was going to happen."

Paige did have a point. I didn't usually go around

giving my cell phone number out to guests. Still, my heart did go out to the woman. I wished I could help her somehow.

"Can I get you anything? There's plenty of hot chocolate." Aunt Thelma had prepared the mixture in the crockpot. She said it was a modern-day cauldron. I had laughed at the reference but told her not to let Connie hear her say such things. The potions master loved her cauldrons.

"Hot chocolate would be nice," Paige took a tentative seat on the couch. I walked over to the hot chocolate bar and scooped two ladles into a mug. Even though I had drunk enough hot chocolate that evening to last a lifetime, I fixed myself a fresh mug. Paige looked like she could use the company.

"Marshmallows?" I asked over my shoulder.

"Yes, please."

I walked over and handed Paige her mug. That's when I noticed she was rubbing a patch of skin on her thumb with her index finger.

"Are you okay?" The patch of skin looked almost black.

"What? Oh, this is nothing. At least I hope it's nothing." Paige took the mug from my hand and took a sip before continuing. "I think it might be frostbite, but I'm not sure. The force of the blast knocked me backward, and when I stood up, it was there. I think a bit of that blue light must have got me. But other than that, I'm fine." Paige clearly didn't want to make a big deal out of it.

"Still, you should probably have Constantine take a look at it. Not tonight," I quickly interjected after noticing Paige's wide eyes, "but tomorrow. I can have her stop by if you're free, just to take a look."

"She's brilliant," Vance chimed in from the counter.

I nodded in agreement. "I'm sure she knows just the perfect cream or potion that can clear that up right away." Or if not, she would work hard to try and figure it out. Speaking of which, I wondered if Sheriff Reynolds had already reached out to see what the healer thought about Mayor Parrish and Rebecca. Hopefully, Constantine would know just what to do.

"Did you, by chance, learn anything tonight? Did the sheriff say what happened?"

"No," Paige looked annoyed. "He had more questions for me, thinking I knew what had happened, but I have no idea. He's hoping Cameron caught something on camera. I told him I hoped so too. Honestly, I don't know why he thinks I had something to do with it." Paige didn't finish her thought. Instead, she took another drink of hot chocolate.

"I don't know. I mean, your sister was pretty rude to you. A lot of people saw it."

"That doesn't mean I froze her into a giant block of ice. Oh my gosh, what kind of sister would I be?"

"No, I hear you. It's just that I'm not surprised the sheriff suspected you. If it makes you feel any better, he's suspected me a time or two."

"Thanks. I guess that does make me feel better, but it still doesn't explain what happened."

"No, I agree." One second there was a blinding light, and the next, it was Snowmageddon. "It makes me wonder if it was an accident or if somebody did this on purpose," I thought aloud.

"You mean like a prank?" Paige asked.

"I hadn't thought of that, but," I looked over at Vance. How often did he have to represent the Robertson boys? Too often if you asked me.

Vance knew what I was thinking. "I'll check in and see what Tommy and his brother were up to tonight. I wouldn't put it past them."

"The Robertson boys are our resident juvenile delinquents," I explained to Paige. She nodded as if every town had a group of kids that were up to no good. Heck, every town probably did have a couple of kids who were up to no good. Teenagers tended to be like that.

"What about Sabrina and Beatrice? They wouldn't freeze the mayor on purpose, but I could see them getting a kick out of making it snow," Vance asked from his side of the lobby.

"Sally took them to Disney World. She was worried they'd pull something." I then turned back to Paige, "The sisters have an odd sense of humor and way of helping."

"They keep you on your toes, that's for sure," Vance added. "With the twins out of the picture, that narrows it down."

"Unless it's not an accident or a prank." I let the gravity of my words sink in. I looked over at Paige. She bit her bottom lip nervously. I wondered what she was thinking.

"What is it? Do you have an idea who might be behind this?"

Paige was quick to erase her expression. "Me? No, I have no idea." Paige thought about her words before speaking. "It's just, like you said, you met my sister. You see the way she acts. She's rude to every-one. I can't tell you how many people she insulted walking around Village Square. Any one of them could have cursed her."

"Unfortunately for her, I think you're right." I agreed with Paige.

Paige stood up abruptly. "I think I'm going to go to bed. Mind if I take this with me?" Paige held up the mug of hot cocoa in reference.

"Not at all. Feel free to top it off before you head on up." I smiled encouragingly at the younger woman.

"Thanks. I'll see you guys tomorrow."

Vance and I waited until Paige was out of earshot before speaking. "It must be tough," Vance said.

I walked over and met him at the counter to face him.

"Which part? Having your sister treat you like trash, or realizing she treats everyone like trash?"

"Both. But the latter makes it pretty hard to narrow down the suspects."

"I hear you. Let's just hope they can turn Mayor Parrish and Rebecca back soon." I felt unsure thinking about the future, and my face showed it.

"It'll be okay," Vance assured me. "I don't know how, but together, we'll figure it out. We always do."

Outside, the snow continued to fall steadily. The fluffy flakes glittered in the fluorescent lighting outside. Watching the flakes was mesmerizing, and I started to feel my eyelids get heavy. Subconsciously, I realized that I must've been waiting to talk to Paige, and now that I had, I was tired. I couldn't stifle the broad yawn that escaped my lips.

"Go on upstairs. I'll stay and keep an eye on things until Percy comes back." Vance suggested once more.

I looked at Vance. It was sweet of him to offer, but he had to be just as tired as I was, which was why I said, "You need sleep too. Why don't we turn the sign off out front and put the phone out. Guests can call if they need anything." I had just said the words when I felt the cold, wet smack of snow hit me on the side of the face. The snowball came out of nowhere. So much for cat-like reflexes. "Percy!" It had to be the poltergeist. Somehow, Vance managed to duck in the nick of time, and another snowball sailed past and hit the wall behind the registration desk.

Percy chuckled as he materialized. "Darn it, at least I got one of ya."

"On second thought," I said as I used the sleeve of my sweatshirt to dry off my cheek. "Now that Percy's back, he can watch the front. Let's go get some sleep."

FIVE

The following day I got out of bed and shuffled over to the window. Peering out the blinds, I couldn't believe how much snow had fallen. It was easily over a foot deep, and more continued to rain down from the sky. At least the snowflakes seemed smaller now. It looked like silver glitter sprinkling down with the way the tiny flakes sparkled in the sunlight. Outside of my bedroom, the apartment was quiet. There was no sign of Vance or my aunt. The latter wasn't surprising, Aunt Thelma was downstairs working, but last night had been a surprise. I couldn't believe Vance had agreed to stay. His bed at home had to be more comfortable than sleeping on the couch, but I was thankful that he hadn't put up a fight. I didn't want to have to worry about him driving through the snowstorm in the dead of night. I liked knowing he was safe and close by.

I walked over to the kitchen to grab a cup of coffee and looked at the time. I was surprised it was already eleven o'clock. I rubbed my eyes to double-check the time. Yep, it was after eleven, alright. I guess that's what I got for staying up until after three in the morning. I yawned and rubbed the sleep out of my eyes. It didn't feel like I had gotten eight hours of sleep. Hopefully, some coffee would help. That's when I spotted Vance's note on the counter.

"I'm headed home to get cleaned up. I'll be back shortly. See you soon." I reread the note and wondered what time Vance had left. Too bad he didn't time stamp it. For all I knew, he'd be knocking on the door in the next ten minutes. Guess I better hurry up and get ready. With a fresh cup of coffee in hand, I set out to do just that.

Twenty minutes later, I was downstairs in the lobby, saying good morning to my aunt. Aunt Thelma looked bright-eyed behind the registration desk. It took me a minute to realize what she was smiling at. Outside, guests were marveling at the snow. Children tossed armfuls into the air while others ran around laughing.

"Isn't it beautiful? I haven't seen snow like this in thirty years. Not since the last time I was in

Manhattan in January." Aunt Thelma's smile grew wider.

I looked out the sliding glass door past the deck and onto the lake. "Are people ice-skating?"

"It's amazing what you can conjure." Aunt Thelma motioned to the wicker baskets by the door. She had one for hats, one for mittens, and one for scarves. Guests had all the winter gear they needed to get outside and have some fun. "I'm out of skates, but I can always order more," she remarked.

I turned away from the lively scene and got down to business. "Is there any talk of what happened?"

"Oh, there's plenty of talk." Aunt Thelma rolled her eyes. "Just no one knows the truth. It's all speculation."

"Did Cameron come back?"

Aunt Thelma thought for a moment. "The cameraman?"

"Mm-hmm."

"Now that I don't know. I didn't see him last night, and I haven't seen him this morning."

"We didn't see him last night either. Vance and I stayed up until after three, and I talked to Paige when she came back."

"How is she holding up?"

"Okay. I think she's a bit shook up."

"I don't blame her. It's awful what happened," Aunt Thelma agreed.

Just then, the one and only Stormy Evans from Witch News Network walked through the door. Now, Stormy Evans I knew. She had been to Silverlake a time or two to cover big events. Another young woman trailed in after her. But it didn't seem like they were together from how they kept their distance. The other woman formed a line behind Stormy.

"Good morning! I was hoping you had a spare room for me," Stormy said.

"Welcome back, Miss Evans. Let me see what we have." Aunt Thelma clicked away on the keyboard. I knew we had a bit of a scramble with people checking in and out last night, but I assumed we had open rooms. It turned out I was right. "Ground-floor okay with you?" My aunt asked the reporter.

"Whatever you have, works."

Aunt Thelma finished checking in Stormy while I motioned for the other woman to come forward.

"Hello, how can I help you?"

"I don't suppose you have room for Megan Mulroney, lead reporter for the Yuletide Times?" Megan gave a winning smile.

I'd never heard of the Yuletide Times, but I had a feeling we'd have plenty of reporters rolling into town to cover the story. Silverlake had its fair share of magical mishaps, but as far as I knew, this was the first time it was broadcast on national television.

"I think we probably do. Do you just need one bed?"

"Yep, that's all."

"Okay, hang on a second." I copied my aunt from a moment ago and clicked through our reservation system, quickly finding an open room. "Second floor good with you?"

"That would be perfect."

It took me a minute to realize that Stormy was waiting to talk with me. She stood off to the side, waiting to catch my attention. I wasn't on a first-name basis with the reporter, and before that moment, I had no idea she even knew I existed. I quickly wrapped up checking in Megan and then gave Stormy my full attention. The reporter flashed her crystal blue eyes at me. With shiny, long, black hair, porcelain smooth skin, and captivating eyes, Stormy looked like a celebrity reporter.

"I heard through the grapevine that you might know where Rebecca and Mayor Parrish are. I was hoping you could help me. Off the record, of course." Stormy leaned in. "Don't worry. I never reveal my sources." Stormy attempted to charm me with the winning smile, but I could instantly tell it was fake. You can't fake authenticity. Megan, who had been ready to grab her bags and walk down the hall, stopped to listen to my answer as well. I don't know why Stormy thought I would know any details. That probably was why she was a reporter.

Aunt Thelma began to speak, but I interrupted. My aunt meant well, but I couldn't be sure what she'd say. I didn't think Luke would want Stormy at the candy shop, and I was afraid Aunt Thelma would reveal the location. It would only make it harder to reverse the curse if the whole world knew where Mayor Parish and Rebecca were.

"I'm not sure. The last I heard was the morgue." I made a face to say what I thought about that. I saw Megan mouth the word morgue and then shake her head.

"They're not dead, are they?" Stormy's face lit up, and not in horror as you'd expect. More like excitement at the turn of events.

"Oh gosh, no. They just needed someplace to keep them frozen. Not a lot of options around here."

Stormy looked disappointed. "No, I suppose not."

I shrugged my shoulders. "The sheriff thought it would be the safest place until this was all sorted out.

"Right, well, thank you," Stormy replied with the fake smile once more in place. Then she left us to go to her room.

"Sorry, I wish I could be more help." I didn't dare look over at my aunt as I said those words for fear I wouldn't be able to keep a straight face. Vance returned at that moment. As he walked through the front door, he stomped the snow off his boots on the black welcome mat.

"It's starting to come down out there again." Vance brushed the snow off his shoulder. "Faster than the town Council can magic it away." Outside, the glittering snow had reverted to big fat flakes once more.

"Maybe I can help," Megan said from behind us. I hadn't even realized that the young woman was still standing there. "Sorry, I didn't mean to eavesdrop, but I'm pretty good with snow removal charms."

"I didn't know there was more than one," I remarked.

"Oh yeah, there's loads. Sometimes you need a fire charm to melt the ice. Other times, a wind charm does the trick. Especially for the light, fluffier stuff. We see it all in Mount Holly."

"Mount Holly. Why does that place sound famil-iar?" I turned to Vance and Aunt Thelma for the answer.

Megan beat them to it. "It's the village of everlasting winter and Yuletide cheer. Everyone's visited at least once or twice."

Everyone, apparently, except for me.

"You'd love it," Aunt Thelma said.

"Everyone does," Megan agreed. "The scenery is beautiful. The people are hospitable. And you couldn't ask for a village with more Christmas spirit."

"You know, I've never been," I said.

"You haven't?" Vance looked surprised. "They have some of the best ski trails I've ever hit. Highly recommend," Vance added.

"And it's Christmas all year?" I asked.

Megan nodded. "It's all part of the charm."

Christmas three hundred and sixty-five days a year? I wasn't sure I could handle that. But I would be up for a visit. Maybe not in the dead of winter, though.

"The charms are great and all, but why are they even necessary? I was hoping we'd have some answers by now," Aunt Thelma remarked.

I was thinking the same thing, but I didn't want to say anything in front of Megan, especially knowing she was a reporter. I didn't want any of our speculations to end up in the Yuletide Times.

"I'm sure we'll have answers soon," I said with a reassuring smile, hoping my aunt would understand.

"About those charms," Vance said to Megan.

"Oh, let me drop my bags off, and then I'll show you. Just give me a minute."

While Megan ran off to do just that, I scoped out the winter gear Aunt Thelma had picked up. If I were going to be cleaning the sidewalks, I would be warm doing it.

I tugged a white knitted stocking cap over my ears and found a pair of matching mittens. I thought a scarf would be overkill until a gust of whipped across the patio out back, billowing a cloud of snow with it. I reached for a scarf and wrapped it around my neck two times, folding the ends inside to keep it nice and snug.

True to her word, Megan showed us a couple of tricks and charms for removing the snow.

"My favorite is a fire charm. Handle it right, and it'll melt everything in site. Works great for cleaning off your car and driveway. Just point your wand at the snow and say, "El Fotio." Megan demonstrated. With a swish and a flick of her wrist, an orange stream of fire appeared at the end of her wand. "Obviously, you don't want to point your wand at anyone when trying this one out."

"You think it's better than an infiro charm?" Vance asked Megan.

"A bit safer, I think. I usually use infiro when lighting a fire. This flame's not as strong."

Not as strong? I liked the sound of that. Vance lit his wand like Megan's, and I thought I might as well give it a try.

Reluctantly, I withdrew my wand and cleared my throat, "El Fotio," I said, a bit unsure of myself. If you knew my history with magic, you'd understand why. A small spark flicked out of my wand before finally catching at the tip. My flame was nowhere near as impressive as Megan's torch. Even Vance looked like a master fire charm worker. Mine was more like a candle flame. I'd have to crawl on the sidewalk to get it to do any good.

I blew the flame away, muddled up my courage, and tried again.

"El Fotio!" I commanded with more bravado than I'd anticipated.

WHOOSH!

A flame erupted from my wand and pulled me forward. It was as if someone had lit a rocket, and I was holding onto the tail.

"How do I control this thing?" I yelled. Panic filled my voice and my body. I ran to keep up with the momentum, trying to control which way the flame went. I managed to melt the snow off two cars, half the lawn, and a mulberry bush before Vance caught up with me.

"Stasi!" He shouted. A red streak burst from his

wand and hit me square between the shoulders. Normally, I hated stunning charms. There was nothing like having your free will stripped from you in an instant. It's like having the wind knocked out of you, and your muscles freeze at the same time. But today, I welcomed it. I stood there stuck in place with my wand outstretched in my hand. A three-foot crackling red flame blazed into the sky.

Vance quickly caught up and extinguished my wand. "Sorry, love, it's the only thing I could think of."

The spell wore off within ten seconds, and I was free to move again.

"No, that's alright. Smart thinking." I cleared my throat, embarrassed after what had just happened.

"Okay, then. Maybe you should stick with a wind charm?" Megan offered helpfully.

"Maybe I'll just stick with a shovel," I replied dryly. But truthfully, the shovels that Aunt Thelma had conjured from Witch-Mart were more than sufficient. I stuck with what I knew, picked up the silver shovel's black handle, and got to work scraping the slushy mess off the sidewalk.

Vance soon followed suit and Megan disappeared back inside.

"I didn't want to ask in front of Megan, but have

you heard anything?" I plopped a shovelful off to the side where the sidewalk met the lawn.

"Nothing good," Vance copied me with the motion, emptying his shovel. "I ran into Constantine at the gas station. There's not a magical medical remedy that she's ever heard of. She's reaching out to her colleagues, but all signs point to a curse."

The edge of my shovel continued to scrape across the concrete. "I keep thinking about how upset Mayor Parrish will be when she finds out what happened. It ruined last night. She was so excited to showcase Silverlake too. She'll be crushed when she finds out."

"If we ever thaw her out." Vance's expression was grim.

"Don't say that. Didn't you tell me last night that we'd figure this out?" I stopped shoveling and looked up at Vance.

"You're right. Forget I said anything."

"Not only that, but Mayor Parrish will never let us forget how long it took us to unfreeze her. The sooner we can figure this out, the better."

"Maybe if we knew who was responsible, we could get them to tell us how to break the curse."

"That's a good idea. We know that Rebecca was nasty to Paige."

"She was rude to a lot of people," Vance clarified.

"You're right. She even insulted Mayor Parrish. Twice."

"Wonder if any of her enemies followed her here? Maybe they wanted to see her demise on national television."

My eyes lit up. "You mean to embarrass her?"

"It's worth looking into."

"You might be onto something. Maybe Paige could help us. Being Rebecca's assistant, she would know as well as anyone who didn't like Rebecca. I know I started to ask her about it last night, but we need to think outside of Silver Lake."

"There are a lot of people from out of town here right now."

"Exactly. Okay, so that's one avenue we can explore. What else?" Vance and I continued to shovel while we thought.

Vance stopped clearing his pathway for a moment and said, "What if Rebecca wasn't the target, but Silverlake was? Who would be the suspects then?"

"So, instead of someone wanting to make Rebecca look bad, they wanted to make Silverlake look bad?"

"That's what I'm thinking."

"Okay, I can buy that. But who doesn't like us?" The rivaling mayor from the nearby town was no longer a problem. Other than that, I was drawing a blank.

"A sore losing town, perhaps? Silverlake won the party last night. Who were the other towns we were up against?"

"Oh, I don't even know. Good question. But you're right. Maybe one of them turned out to be a sore loser and sought out revenge." It seemed a bit extreme, but I never claimed to understand the motives behind the things that some people did.

"After we're done here, I'll head down to the sheriff's department and see what I can find out. Maybe Deputy Jones will tell me something." We had made good time cleaning off the sidewalks. Now, if only the snow would stop falling.

"That's a good idea. Share our theories with the deputy and see what he thinks. Plus, there was that woman." I twisted my lips to the side while I tried to remember her in detail.

"What woman?"

"Don't you remember? She stood next to us and made a couple of comments about Rebecca. I couldn't tell if she was amused, disgusted, or impressed. And then, when the snowstorm hit, the woman laughed. I don't know. It's probably nothing. For all I know, the woman was in shock like the rest of us."

"But you still want to check her out."

I nodded. "She was dressed in comfortable clothes, which was why she stuck out."

"She wasn't there to party."

"No, I'd say not formally. And she wasn't a local either." I was pretty sure I could tell the locals from the tourists now. It hadn't taken long being back in Silverlake to know who was who.

"So, the question is, what was she doing there then?"

"Exactly. Like I said, it's probably nothing, but I want to track her down."

"She's not a guest here?" Vance motioned with his head to the three-story inn behind us.

"Not that I know of. Last night was the first time I'd seen her, and I checked in most of our guests, but I'll put the word out to the staff to keep an eye out." I wasn't sure if the weekend help would still make it in, but I'd describe the woman to my aunt and Percy. The weekend crew was primarily high schoolers who had picked up hours here and there. If the roads were icy, though, I didn't want them to risk driving in this weather. "I'm going to go check in with Aunt Thelma and see if she thinks we should call off any staff and then pop over to the bed and breakfast. Maybe Shannon knows who I'm talking about."

"If she's not a guest there, maybe she was just passing through."

"Maybe, although I was hoping I could catch up with her." If anything, to ease my suspicions.

"Roger and Diane sure picked a good time to honeymoon," Vance said.

I had to agree. My back would be sore come tomorrow morning shoveling all this thick, wet snow. It looked like I would have to switch to using my wand and a charm sooner than I had anticipated, which made me question how Aunt Thelma would have ever managed this snow if Vance and I weren't in town. "You know how much I'm looking forward to going away, right?" I stood still for a moment to capture Vance's full attention.

"But you're not comfortable leaving Silverlake like this." Vance read my mind.

I shook my head.

"That's okay because neither am I. Which is why we need to double our efforts and solve this mystery so you and I can go away for a nice relaxing vaca-tion." Vance closed the space between us as he said those last four words. I welcomed the closeness. Vance bent low to give me a sweet kiss.

"I really hope we figure this mystery out soon," I said, savoring the moment.

"That makes two of us."

SIX

Vance and I parted ways soon after. As promised, he headed to the sheriff's department, and I borrowed Aunt Thelma's car to drive around the other side of the lake to the B&B. The bed-and-breakfast was technically in the business district. Unlike this side of the lake, where Village Square and the restaurants were, the bed-and-breakfast was on the same block as the church, courthouse, and City Hall. That was because the B&B was the old mayor's mansion. But after Mayor Parrish was elected, she refused to give up her luxury condo for an old drafty Victorian home. The mayor had no problem auctioning the house off to the highest bidder, which happened to be Shannon Prescott. It took a couple of years, but after fixing the grand home up, Shannon was now open for business.

It took a moment or two to remember how to drive on ice. Even though I had lived in Chicago, I'd only owned a car for a short period of time after realizing how expensive it was to park the blasted thing. Still, as I slipped and slid it through Silverlake's one and only intersection, it all started to come back to me. "Turn into the slide," I reminded myself as I regained control of the wheel. It almost felt like playing bumper cars. You know those electric cars at carnivals? I wondered how many fender benders would happen before the snowstorm ended.

Shannon had the storybook Victorian painted in an ivory shade of white. The home had high turrets, pilaster columns, and the best front porch in all of Silverlake. Maybe even all of Georgia. I parked at the road, careful not to bury the tires in the snow that had piled up at the curb, and carefully walked to the front door. Shannon was on the porch, attempting to deice the steps with her wand. Behind her, propped up against the door, was a shovel.

"Now, you look like me twenty minutes ago," I remarked.

Shannon stepped aside to let me pass. "I know, this is ridiculous." Shannon blew her bangs out of her eyes. Her long, blonde hair was pulled up in a high ponytail, and her nose was running from the cold weather. I knew the feeling well.

"Here, let me help you." I didn't wait for Shannon to protest. Instead, I grabbed the shovel off the porch and started scraping off the sidewalk. In no time, we had the walkways clear. Of course, that's when the snow kicked back up. It would only be a matter of minutes before Shannon would have to clear the way once more.

"I don't even know why I bother. It's not like I have any guests."

"You don't?"

"You do?"

"Yeah, quite a few, surprisingly. Although, some are probably here against their will."

Shannon cocked her head as if she wasn't following me.

"A couple are reporters. I'm pretty sure their employers are the ones that sent them here."

"Fair enough. I had a packed house, but once that snowstorm hit, my guests cleared out. Not that I blame them." Shannon visibly shivered. "Thanks for your help with this. Is there something you need? Or did you just stop by to clear my walkway? Not that I'm complaining," Shannon quickly clarified.

"Actually, I was wondering if a woman was staying here, but it sounds like that answer is no."

"She might've been at one point. What did she look like?"

I went on to describe the woman with her honeyed skin tone, dark corkscrew curls, and multicolored patchwork coat.

"No, she doesn't sound familiar. Was there someone else with her? All I usually have here are couples."

"That's the thing. I'm not sure. I didn't see anyone with her, but that doesn't mean she was in town alone. Oh well, it's no big deal. It was probably nothing anyway."

"Still, I'll keep my eye out and let you know if I see anyone who fits that description."

"Great, thanks. I appreciate it."

Seeing it was Saturday, I decided to stick with my usual routine and stop in and visit Misty at the bookstore. Saturday mornings were always my time off, and I loved nothing more than stopping in the bookstore to waste the morning away with a good book and friendly conversation.

I held my breath as I drove around the back side of the lake, and Wishing Well Park came into view. If I'd thought the inn had received a lot of snow, it was nothing compared to the park. The white reception tent was encased in ice. Giant icicles hung off the support poles, their tips disappearing into the snow piled on the ground. Fire shot out of the hired workers' wands as they deiced the tent and surrounding tables in an attempt to break the reception area down. Yellow crime scene tape and a set of sawhorses sectioned off the countdown ball and surrounding platform, acting as a barricade.

Stormy Evans stood in front of the barricade. She wore a red wool coat, a fur-trimmed hat, and black leather gloves. She held on to her microphone with one hand and motioned behind her with the other. I noticed Cameron was behind the camera. I'm sure he had told the Sheriff everything he knew, but I was curious to hear things straight from the source.

Unlike most Saturday mornings, parking was plentiful today. I was able to park in the main lot right up front by the bookstore. Misty was outside, clearing her sidewalks. It looked like she was attempting a wind charm with how the snow billowed around her. Unfortunately, all the spell did was seem to create more of a mess, blowing the snow onto the cobblestone path that led over to the tavern. Misty stopped working for a moment and looked up at the sky as if cursing the clouds as they continued to rain snowflakes down. I waved my hand in the air to get her attention. Misty nodded back. I then held my mittened hand up in the shape of a C and did the universal sign for getting a drink. "You want one?" I hollered across the parking lot.

"Make it a double!" Misty shouted back.

"Vicki too?" I yelled back.

Misty gave me a thumbs up.

I nodded that I understood and had turned to head in the opposite direction toward the bakery when I almost lost it. My foot hit a piece of ice just so, and I lost my balance. Thankfully, my left foot didn't land on ice, and I was able to stabilize myself after doing a one-legged wobble.

"Oh, my word." I slapped my hand to my heart. Mental images of twisting and breaking my ankle came to mind. I would have to be more careful, or I'd ruin my vacation with Vance yet. I carefully walked the rest of the way to the bakery, keeping my eyes on the ground and on the lookout for more ice. I debated for a split second, pulling my wand out and attempting the fire charm again, but I'd probably burn down half of Village Square if I tried. No, I was safer taking it slow.

It was when I was coming out of the bakery that I ran into Luke. He looked exhausted. He had dark purple circles under his eyes. His black hair was a tousled mess. And his face was way past a five o'clock shadow.

"Are you okay?" I reached out my hand to steady him. I held the drink carrier in the other hand with three coffees to-go.

"I look that bad, huh?"

"I'm sorry." I grimaced and removed my hand. "I thought you were dead on your feet for a moment there."

Luke rubbed his eyes. "I am dead on my feet. Amber's been at the shop, and I was afraid to leave her alone. She said she was guarding the freezer, but she ate me out of inventory. Don't even get me started on her opinions. She had something to say about everything I made."

"And I thought the twins were bad with their chocolate concoctions."

"I'd take the twins in my kitchen any day over Amber. She's bossy and rude, and if she had eaten another bonbon, my head would've exploded."

"Yikes, that bad."

"You know that expression, no good deed goes unpunished? That's the way I feel right now."

"I'm sorry. Want me to stop by and keep an eye on her for a bit so you can go home and get some rest?" Not that my presence would go over well.

"No, she left, thankfully. Deputy Jones was sent over in her place. I'll head home as soon as I make more chocolates. In the meantime, I'm going to grab an extra-large coffee." Luke motioned to the bakery behind us with his head.

"Okay, good luck. And I hope you get some rest soon."

"Thanks."

When I got to the bookstore, it was dead. There wasn't anyone else in sight besides Vicki, who was rearranging the New Year displays, again.

"Where's Misty?" I asked Vicki.

"Here!" Misty said, coming out from the back room with a box full of books. "I've been meaning to go through this old inventory forever. Guess there's no time like the present." Misty dropped the box of books down at her feet.

"Coffee?" I handed one to Misty and one to Vicki as well.

"Did you end up getting any sleep last night?" Misty asked me.

"I did, although it doesn't feel like it. What about you?"

Misty blushed. Vicki and I both laughed at the unexpected reaction.

"I had a very nice New Year's Eve, thank you very much. Daniel and I stayed up all night talking, and it was nice, that's all."

"Uh-huh," I replied dryly.

"They stayed up all night talking," Vicki replied.

"Stop it. We did. But now I'm tired, and with the snow coming down like it is, I'm not sure it's worth it to stay open." Misty yawned.

"I take it you haven't heard any news then?" I asked the duo.

"No, have you?" Vicki asked.

"No, afraid not," I confessed.

"Oh, but did you see the instant replays? They've gone viral." Misty retrieved her smartphone from her pocket and quickly brought up a video. "There's a bunch of footage from last night. People were recording ringing in the new year when it hit." Misty held her phone horizontal for me to look at the screen. She hit the play triangle, and we watched as people clapped and cheered on the screen, counting down the seconds until the new year would strike. I held my breath, knowing what happened next. The moment the ball hit the base of the pole, a blinding blue light flashed onto the screen. The phone picked up the commotion of shrieks and screams, and then the video went dead. It looked as if the recorder had dropped the phone.

"There's more, loads more, but they all show the same thing." Misty re-pocketed her phone.

"It makes me wonder, what was cursed? The ball itself or something else?" I thought aloud.

"I have no idea," Misty replied.

Vicki opened up a book from the side table. "I was going through books to see what we had on curses. It could be a time curse that went off at a given second in time. I'm not exactly sure how they work, though. The physics is a bit beyond me." If the physics were beyond Vicki, it would let be light years ahead of my understanding.

"Vance and I were thinking that instead of trying to solve the curse, we should find out who's responsible for it and get them to solve it."

Vicki closed the book in her hands. "I like that plan. This book is giving me a headache."

"You and Vance have any other ideas?" Misty asked.

"Well, we talked about who might have it out for Silverlake. Seeing we won the party last night, one of the other towns might have sabotaged us."

Vicki scrunched her nose, and Misty looked skeptical. "That might be a bit of a stretch," she said.

"I agree. The other thought was that somebody had it out for Rebecca. Unfortunately, it's a tough list to narrow down who that might be. We're going to check in with Paige and see where to start. Maybe someone followed her here."

"They might not have had to follow her. They might be from here."

"That too," I conceded.

"Why, what do you know?" Misty asked, taking the conversation in a different direction than what I was thinking.

"I think you should start at the campground," Vicki said matter-of-factly.

"The campground?" Misty and I said in unison.

"What was it now, eight years ago? I'd have to do the math, but Rebecca's been here before. She was a volunteer for summer camp. I use that term loosely. She mostly flirted with the counselors and used the experience as a resume builder. Rebecca didn't care about the kids one bit. I was one of the head counselors back then, and I couldn't even get her to help with craft time. Occasionally, she'd lifeguard, but I couldn't be sure she was actually watching the kids and not just working on her tan. She said she'd never come back, and I told her that was fine by me because she wasn't welcome back."

"Ouch," Misty said.

Vicki shrugged. "Trust me. I wasn't the only one who felt that way. I was surprised when I saw Michael talking to her in town yesterday."

"Michael Strato?" Misty asked.

Vicki nodded. I knew Michael's family owned the campground, and if I thought about it, he was probably the same age as Rebecca. "They had a bit of a falling out. I don't know all the details, but Michael might be willing to talk." Again, Vicki shrugged.

Just then, Megan popped into the bookstore. Just like the kids outside, Megan looked like she was having fun. She had a gray stocking cap tugged down over her curls. Her cheeks were bright pink, and her face lit up with a broad smile when she spotted us. "You don't have a stable around here, do you?"

"A stable?" Misty looked bewildered.

"For horses and a sleigh?" Megan clarified.

"Mr. McCormick, maybe? He has hay and a tractor. Does he have horses?" Vicki looked to me to answer.

"I don't think so." I hadn't been out to the property in quite some time but didn't think Mr. McCormick kept livestock.

"Hayrides?" Megan seemed to think for a moment. "That might work. Thanks!"

Misty gave me a look as soon as Megan walked out the door, and Vicki went to re-shelve her book on curses. "There's something not right about that woman," Misty remarked.

"I don't know. She seems nice. And she really loves the snow."

"Exactly, who loves the snow? Nobody." I think what Misty meant to say was nobody who lived down south. That was one of the benefits of living in Georgia. "You don't think she orchestrated all this to draw people to that Christmas town of hers, do you?"

"I don't know. I never thought of that. I've never been to Mount Holly, have you?"

"No, but they were runner-up to the WNN contest." Misty raised her eyebrows to let the implications hang in the air.

Mrs. Potts appeared out of nowhere. "I didn't know you were here," I said in surprise at seeing my former second-grade teacher.

"Oh, I came in the back."

"Mighty brave of you to venture out in this weather," Misty added.

"I grew up in Nebraska. This is nothing. What were you guys just talking about?"

"Mount Holly, have you ever been?" I asked.

"Oh yes, George and I vacationed there on our honeymoon." George was Mrs. Potts' former spouse. He had passed away probably twenty years ago. "It's a lovely village up in the mountains, full of evergreens and crisp snow. They don't allow cars there, you know. It's like being transported to another time."

"I didn't know that." Misty looked to me for confirmation.

"Me either."

"Oh yes, you have to check in your car before you enter the town. And they have horses and sleighs that pick you up and take you right through the center of town to the hotel. It's quite magical."

"Sounds like it." And it made a bit more sense why Megan was looking for a horse and sleigh.

"A horse and sleigh, you don't say?" Misty's comment was directed toward me.

"You don't think it just makes it more convenient to travel through town?" I said to Misty.

She looked at me skeptically. "Are you kidding me? She's probably telling everyone that if they love this, just wait until they come to Mount Holly."

Mrs. Potts looked confused.

"Sorry," I apologized to my former teacher for having a side conversation. "Mount Holly does sound like a beautiful place. More and more, I think I need to check it out." And by check it out, I meant looking closer at Megan and what her motives may be. But first, I had a campground to visit. "Okay, well, guess I'll be off to see what I can find out. In the meantime, you two don't work too hard."

Misty snorted. As far as I knew, Mrs. Potts was the only customer they'd had all morning.

SEVEN

I glanced across the street back at the park when I left the bookstore and noticed Stormy Evans was no longer reporting. Now, I know I had places to go and people to see, but I couldn't ignore the itch to go across the street and take a closer look at the scene of the crime.

I headed across the street with my mittens tucked into my coat pockets and my face buried into my scarf. I didn't think it was possible, but the air felt colder with every step I took as if I was inching closer and closer to the North Pole. The air grew drier, and my exposed cheeks stung from the bitter air.

Around me, workers continued to dismantle the reception site. They were bundled up in thick overalls and flannel coats. Someone had built an enchanted fire in the center of the park. Green and purple flames swirled amongst the logs. A steady stream of smoke rose into the air. I could see the heat waves from where I stood and hoped it was warming the area where they worked a little. The main stage, the one Daniel had performed on, had already been dismantled, and they were packing it away on a nearby truck.

Flames erupted from the tip of the worker's wands as they melted the ice-coated poles of the over-sized tent. It looked like someone had mastered the fire charm, and it wasn't me. That being said, the workers didn't look at me twice as I snooped around the park. They obviously were trying to get their job done and get out of there as soon as possible. I didn't blame them.

Eventually, I came to stand before the oversized countdown ball. In the daylight, it looked completely unremarkable. Every bulb appeared intact, and I didn't even see a scratch on the silver, reflective exterior. I leaned over the orange and white striped barricade and tilted my head to the side, trying to see where the ball made an impact with the stage. I wondered if anything was underneath it. Perhaps a detonator that could've set off the chain of events when the ball dropped onto it. It was the only conclusion my mortal mind could come up with. I crouched low to look under the barricade and check out the scene from another angle. By my calculations, the stage was about three feet off the ground, just enough for Rebecca to report over the crowd and for everyone to see the ball. The clear, blue ice which had transformed Mayor Parrish and Rebecca into ice sculptures spilled over the edge of the platform, making a three-inch-thick lip. That was the extent of the ice. It was a relatively small radius, given the shocking aftermath.

When I stood up, something reflective in the ice hit my eyes. I lowered myself closer to the ground again and slowly stood. For the second time, something blue caught the reflection of the sun. It was hard to tell what it was, given that it blended in with the ice, but there was something encased inside. I looked to either side of me. The workers continued their tasks, and no one else was on site. Without a second thought, I ducked under the barrier and stepped closer to the platform. I used my mitten-covered hand to brush the ice and clear away the wayward flakes to see what had caused the reflection.

"Step away with your hands up," Amber said from behind me.

I froze and closed my eyes. "You have to be kidding me."

"What's that?" Amber shot back from behind me. In the next moment, I heard Amber talking on her radio. "Hey Daddy, yeah, I got someone all right. I just caught Angelica Nightingale red-handed. Want me to bring her in?"

I whipped around and shot daggers at Amber. "That's not necessary. How about you come over here. I want to show you something."

"Don't try to change the subject," Amber snapped back.

"I'm serious. There is something here in the ice. It might be important."

Amber was back to talking on her two-way radio. "The sheriff says you need to step away from the platform and answer a couple of questions." Amber turned away from me to carry on her conversation in private. I started to do as she requested when I spotted another piece of reflective material on the ground. Without thinking, I swooped down and picked it up. It was a chunk of iridescent blue glass. I pocketed the piece and met Amber on the other side of the barrier.

"Listen, this might be important," I started to say. Amber held up her index finger to silence me. I fought hard not to roll my eyes.

It was then, standing there waiting for Amber to lecture me, that I spotted the mystery woman from last night. It had to be her. The woman was wearing the same patchwork coat as before. I watched as she headed up the path, disappearing into Village Square. It was hard to say where she went after that, given the dozens of shops she could slip into.

"Hang on. I'll be right back." I turned to run and catch up with the woman when Amber caught me by the sleeve of my coat.

"You're not going anywhere until you answer my questions."

"There's someone I really need to talk to. Trust me. I'm not going far." I pulled back on my coat.

Amber didn't budge.

"I don't think you understand the situation you're in. You know I could have you arrested, right?"

"Which is what I was trying to explain to you. There's something stuck in the ice over here. It might be important. That's all I was doing. I was checking it out." I looked across the parking lot to where I last saw the woman, and already I had no idea where she went. At least I knew she was still in town. I tried not to sigh in frustration. Instead, I regained my composure and focused back on Amber. "Do you want to come see what I'm talking about?"

Amber looked conflicted. On the one hand, she didn't want to do anything I suggested. But on the other, I knew she was curious about what I had discovered.

"Fine, but there better be something there, or I'm

hauling you in." Amber dropped my coat sleeve, and I led her over to the item in question.

I pointed at the object underneath the ice. Amber bent low to take a closer look. "So what? It looks like a piece of glass." Amber was not impressed by my discovery.

"It might be important."

Amber looked skeptical. "I don't see how. It's more like someone was careless with their cocktail last night. We'll probably find glass in the park for weeks. A bit reckless if you ask me. Not sure why they had to go all fancy with the glasses."

I wasn't so sure. Especially given the location of the glass and the fact that it was light blue. I didn't remember seeing colored glassware last night. I kept my thoughts to myself. "Suit yourself. I just thought the police might want to know about it."

Amber rolled her eyes. "How about you save the investigating for the professionals. You don't see me at the inn telling you how to manage your guests, do you?"

I could've said a dozen different things about how Amber had no idea how to run a business or be hospitable, but instead, I smiled and feigned agreement. "Speaking of the inn, I better get back. Until next time." I didn't wait for Amber to try and stop me again. I turned around, slipped under the barrier, and jogged across the parking lot toward my car.

I had almost made it when I felt a snowball pummel me on the back of my coat. My first instinct was that it was Percy. I even had his name on my lips when I turned around to confront the culprit and found myself in the middle of a snowball fight. Adults and children alike had gathered on the lawn surrounding Village Square, going all out. Somehow, I had gotten caught in the crosshairs in my quick escape from Amber.

"Hey!" I shouted, covering my head with my hands and ducking for cover. I might not have been the intended target, but I still got hit with three or four snowballs. "It's going to be like that, huh?" I hollered to no one in particular. I ducked down and used the neighboring car for cover. I spotted Clemmie hiding behind a cluster of pine trees, directing the troops. It looked like kids versus adults, well, except for Clemmie, who was on the kid side, and the kids were clearly winning.

By the time I made it safely inside my car, I was covered in snow. I looked at my reflection in the rearview mirror. My cheeks were pink, and my jeans were soaking wet. In fact, my mittens were too. And I was cold, so very cold. "Okay, change of plans. First,

I'll head back to the inn and change. Then I'll head to the campground."

We needed to catch the culprit as soon as possible before hot chocolate was ruined to me forever. I had drunk more of the delicious chocolatey drink in the past twelve hours than I had in the previous twelve months. I wasn't a big tea drinker, but I was willing to give it a shot. There was only so much hot chocolate and coffee a woman could drink before she got tired of it.

With my clothes changed and the car's heat cranked up to high, I drove the short distance to the campground. The campground was in an isolated and underdeveloped area between the inn and the business district. On an average day, it took about a fifteen-minute walk down the Enchanted Trail to reach the campground. We knew today wasn't an average day, and I had no idea concerning the trail's condition or if it was even passable. I turned off the main drag onto the long, bumpy driveway of Hidden Hills Campground. Speaking of being accessible, if the snow continued to fall at the rate it was presently coming down, the campground would be isolated in no time. The car bumped down the snow-packed dirt road. Thankfully, someone had blazed the trail before me.

I bypassed the check-in point, seeing no one was at the small outpost anyway, and continued to drive on through to the back of the park where the Strato family lived.

Hidden Hills looked like a ghost town. Only two campers remained. They had parked their RVs beside one another. Smoke slowly rose from the metal-ringed fire pit. The rest of the lots were empty. Half-buried tire tracks were all that remained of last night's guests. The scene was night and day from twenty-four hours ago. The campground tended to stay busy year-round due to our mild winters. The holidays were no exception. If anything, this year they were busier.

The Strato's had designed the campground like a grid with streets that ran parallel to one another, with one road that wrapped around the perimeter. I followed the road to the back of the property and found myself at the end of the Strato's driveway. The family lived in an A-frame log cabin home. I saw the man I was looking for right outside, standing next to the detached garage. He was wearing a red stocking cap and a hooded sweatshirt. He swung an ax above his head and brought it down with a blow, cleanly splitting a piece of wood into two. Michael ignored the wood pieces much as he ignored me as I got out of my car.

Michael continued to work, picking up a new log, positioning it just so, and splitting it without looking up. It's not that Michael didn't know I was standing there. He was choosing to ignore me.

"Hey, sorry to bother you. I was wondering if you had a minute to talk."

THWACK!

Another piece split into two.

"Not really." Michael didn't look up but rather continued the task at hand.

"I understand you're busy. This will only take a second. I'm trying to find out everything I can about Rebecca. I want to help her."

Michael scoffed at the mention of Rebecca's name.

I cleared my throat. This was not going well. "You see, if we can find out who caused the snowstorm, we can hopefully get them to unfreeze her and Mayor Parrish." On second thought, I probably should've led with needing to help the mayor over Rebecca. Oh well, I couldn't take back my earlier plea.

Michael stopped moving for the first time since I laid eyes on him. He turned and gave me a level stare. "If you ask me, she got what she deserved. Now she's as frozen as her heart. Now, if you'll excuse me, I got work to do."

That was a dismissal if I ever had received one. As I walked back to my car, I thought that the trip had been a complete waste of time, but then I realized Michael had told me just as much with his actions as he had with his words. Michael did not like Rebecca one bit. And I honestly didn't know him that well. For all I knew, he could very well be the culprit.

EIGHT

I drove back to the inn with a lot on my mind. Michael could be the bad guy. Then again, so could Megan, and what about the mystery woman? There were too many people at play, and I didn't have any evidence on any of them. Well, unless I counted a blue piece of glass as evidence, and that might turn out to be nothing. I had no idea if or how it all tied together, but I was determined to find out.

Back at the inn, I waved at Emily behind the front counter. "I'm surprised you made it in."

"My dad dropped me off. He volunteered to deice Village Square, so it was on the way."

"Oh, good deal then. Have you seen my aunt?"

"I think she's upstairs with Clemmie."

"Perfect, thank you." I bypassed the elevator and jogged up to our private apartment on the third floor. Emily was right. Aunt Thelma and Clemmie were sitting at the dining room table. A teapot rested on the table between them, as did a plate of buttered shortbread.

"Tea?" Clemmie asked when I walked through the door.

"I suppose a cup wouldn't hurt." I took my mittens off and rubbed my hands together. I'd only been back down south for a few months, and already, I was no longer used to the cold weather.

Clemmie poured a cup of tea while my aunt put two shortbread cookies on a saucer, and together they handed me the serving. I sat across the table from them with my aunt sitting at the head of the table.

It was only then that I noticed my aunt's appearance. Her skin was baby smooth, her green eyes were sparkling, and her lips were perfectly outlined in a lovely shade of peach that complimented her skin tone.

She had used a glamour charm once more. "Two days in a row?" I motioned to my aunt's face with a smile. "This wouldn't have anything to do with Mr. Kringle, would it?"

"We'll talk about that in a minute. Why don't you

tell us what's on your mind?" My aunt was ever perceptive.

"You're definitely thinking about something," Clemmie agreed.

"I am. I'm thinking about quite a bit," I confessed. I went on to tell my aunt and her friend all the thoughts swirling around in my head, ending with Rebecca previously working at the campground, and Michael's attitude toward her.

"Hmmm," Clemmie replied, lost in thought.

"You could be onto something," Aunt Thelma agreed.

"I think so too, but I need to know more about Michael and find out if he has an alibi for last night."

"I didn't see him at the party, did you?" My aunt asked Clemmie.

"No, but there were so many people there. I can't say for certain who I did see."

"I agree. Even if Michael was there last night, that doesn't mean much. I need to find out if anyone saw him near the countdown ball, maybe place him at the scene of the crime," I added.

"It would help if we knew what kind of curse we were dealing with," Clemmie stated.

"That reminds me. I found this piece of glass by the ball. There's another one stuck in the ice. Does it mean anything to either one of you?" I walked over and retrieved the fragment from my coat pocket and placed it on the table between them.

Clemmie poked the glass with her finger. "Not off the top of my head. Does it to you?" Clemmie asked Aunt Thelma.

"I'm afraid it doesn't. But I'll keep thinking about it."

I picked the piece of glass up, walked over to the kitchen, and put it on the top shelf in the cupboard. "If you guys think of something, let me know. I'll keep it up here for now. In the meantime, I need to investigate Michael."

"He mostly runs things at the campground nowadays, but his grandparents still live on the property. You're going to want to talk to Hammish or Gertie," Aunt Thelma said.

I looked up at the ceiling while I thought. How would I arrange a run-in with either one of the elder Solano's without Michael nearby? I needed to find a way to talk to either one of them one-on-one.

Aunt Thelma read my thoughts. "Gertie's friends with Mrs. Potts, if that helps at all. Maybe she could arrange a get-together."

Clemmie clapped her hands together. "I've got it. They're both Simmering Sisters. Seeing it's the first of the month, they'll be having a meeting tomorrow. I used to be a member, but there was too much cooking and not enough eating. Who has time for that?"

"Any idea where the meeting is being held?" From what I knew, the Simmering Sisters each took turns hosting the meetings at their house.

"Hold on. I can probably find out. I'll get us an invitation, too." Clemmie pulled out her cell phone from her purse. After scrolling through her contact log, she pushed a button and made a call. "Lorraine? Yeah, listen, it's Clemmie. You still having a Simmering Sisters meeting tomorrow? You are? Good. See, the thing is, I'm thinking about joining back up again. That be all right with you? Oh, I know you will all need to vote on it, but I'd like to stop in tomorrow if it's all right. All right then, I'll see you at your place tomorrow at two o'clock. Uh-huh. Bye-bye." Clemmie clicked the end call button and looked at me with a broad smile. "Tomorrow at 2 o'clock at Lorraine's house."

"Impressive," I remarked. "How about I pick you up at 1:30? That is if you don't need the car," I said to Aunt Thelma.

"You go right ahead," My aunt replied.

Clemmie nodded her head. "That'll do just fine."

"Now that that's settled, you want to tell me what

you're up to tonight?" I turned the topic of conversation back on my aunt.

"If you must know, Mayor Kringle is feeling much better, and he's asked me out to dinner."

"Mayor Kringle? You didn't say he was a Mayor."

"I didn't? Well, it's no secret, dear. He's the mayor of that Christmas village, Mount Holly. Remember, we were just talking about it."

"Yes, I remember talking about it, but you didn't mention he was from there. Don't you think it's all too much of a coincidence?"

Clemmie and my aunt looked at me like I had two heads. "The mayor from Mount Holly is here. They're the losing town from the WNN contest. Did you know that part?"

"No, I don't think I knew that," Aunt Thelma wrinkled her nose.

"Then a reporter from their town shows up, our town freezes over, and they think it's the greatest thing ever. It's all just too much of a coincidence."

"He did ask me to go ice skating," Aunt Thelma said more to herself than anyone else.

"It's as if none of this is surprising to him!" I exclaimed.

"I don't know, Thelma. The girl makes a point."

"Well, when you put it that way," Aunt Thelma let her words trail off.

I smacked my hand on the table and leaned back. "You can't go out with him. There's too much we don't know."

"What do you mean? Of course, I have to go out with him! Someone needs to find out more information, and I don't see the man asking you out."

Clemmie snorted.

I glared at Clemmie.

She still smiled.

"It's not funny. It could be dangerous."

"It's not going to be dangerous. We're going out to dinner, and while I'm there, I can find out more about him. Like what brought him into town. It will be fine. Trust me." Aunt Thelma reached across the table and squeezed my hand. I couldn't help the scowl on my face.

"Now you know how we always feel with you rushing out to solve this crime or that one," Clemmie quipped. "It's not fun being on the other side of the equation, is it?"

"No. No, it is not." I turned my attention to my aunt. "Promise me you won't go anywhere alone with the man. Dinner and that is it."

"Yes, ma'am. I suppose you'd like me to call you when I get in."

"Trust me, that won't be necessary." Because I wasn't planning on letting my aunt out of my sight.

"How tired are you?" I said when Misty answered her cell phone.

"Why?" Misty dragged out the question.

"Because that new man my aunt is dating? He's the mayor of Mount Holly."

"Just tell me where you need me to be." This was why I loved Misty. Everyone needed a best friend like her.

"They're going to dinner at The Grove at six o'clock. I want to keep an eye on them."

"I'll be ready by five-thirty."

"Okay, see you then."

Two hours later, Misty and I sat parked across the street from the restaurant. Aunt Thelma and Frederick had picked a booth right up front, and we could see everything through the window.

"She looks like she's having a good time," Misty remarked from the passenger seat.

"For all we know, she's smiling because he's drugged her," I grumbled.

Misty rolled her eyes. "I agree there's a lot of coincidences right now." I started to cut Misty off, but she plowed on, "And you don't believe in coincidences, but we could be wrong about this." Misty motioned with her head to their table. Mayor Kringle reached across the table for Aunt Thelma's hand. She readily met him halfway.

I sighed. "He could be pretending."

"He could be," Misty agreed. "But why go through all the trouble?"

"Because he needs a cover," But even as I said the words, I wasn't too sure. Mayor Kringle could've rode into town, set off the New Year's Eve curse, and left without staying in town a single night. In fact, that's what he should have done if he was the bad guy. Michael, on the other hand, had no place to go. If he ran, he'd look guilty. It was something to think about.

"Look, but don't look." Misty reached across the center console to stop me from whipping around.

"What, what is it?" I craned my neck to see what I was missing inside the restaurant. Visions of Mayor Kringle attempting to abduct my aunt came to mind, but I realized nothing of the sort was happening when I saw them bent low over a menu. From what I could tell, my aunt had finished dinner, and they were thinking about ordering dessert.

"No, across the street. It's that Megan girl."

"The reporter?" I slowly turned to where Misty was pointing.

"Look, she has binoculars! What is she doing?" Misty looked incredulous.

"Is she staking out the restaurant?" I squinted

through the dashboard of Megan's rental. Her car was facing ours on the opposite end of the street.

"I don't know. Maybe she has the same theory as you." Misty raised her eyebrows.

I thought for a moment. "That means, though, if Megan's watching her Mayor, then she didn't set off the curse either."

Misty waved her head from side to side. "I suppose you're right."

"I think I should talk to her."

Misty looked over her shoulder. "Well, that's good because she's headed this way."

"She's what?!" I jumped back in my seat. Sure enough, Megan was making a beeline for our vehicle. She strolled right up to the driver's side window and waved at me through the glass.

I turned on the car and rolled down the window.

"Want to compare notes?" Megan said with a smile.

I didn't even try to fake ignorance. "I think that might be a good idea. How about we meet over at the diner. Do you know where it is?"

"I do. I'll see you there in twenty minutes?"

I nodded my agreement and rolled up the window. Then turned to Misty.

"Well then," my friend remarked.

"To the diner, we shall go." I took one last look at my aunt, reminded myself that she was a strong witch in her own right, and pulled away from the curb.

———

"I heard you have a knack for solving crime," Megan said after Vance's mom, Heather, stopped by with the pitcher of peach tea for Misty and me and a glass of cola for Megan.

"Something like that," I admitted.

"She's just being modest. Angelica's the best there is," Misty replied with a wink.

I turned to my friend. "Stop." I gave her a warning look with my eyes.

Misty shrugged her shoulders. "It's true. You have a knack for solving puzzles. Anyway, what have you uncovered?" Misty asked Megan.

"Not much. I was hoping I'd know a lot more by now," Megan confessed. "At first, I came out to see what Mayor Kringle was up to, and then I couldn't help but try cracking this case."

"And what is Mayor Kringle up to?" Misty flat-out asked.

"He's a good guy. His heart is in the right place,

but his head isn't always. Sometimes his ideas?" Megan shook her head. "Anyway, with that being said, I've got nothing on him. It seems his motives are altruistic."

"How so?" I questioned.

"I found out through Heather," Megan motioned with her head across the diner to where Vance's mom was cashing out a customer, "that he met with Mayor Parrish earlier New Year's Eve to talk about tourism. She said she overheard them talk about what Mount Holly could do to help improve visitor turnout the way you guys have here in Silverlake. Mayor Kringle told me the same thing, but it was nice to hear someone else back up the story. Then, after seeing him dote on your aunt tonight, I can tell that he cares for her, and it's not some cover."

Misty looked over at me. "See?"

I shook my head as if to say, not now. Instead, I said, "I could see that. So, Mayor Kringle comes to Silverlake to see how we run things, and he is staying a few extra days because he hit it off with my aunt."

"That's pretty much it," Megan replied. "And I have to be honest. It's not good for business to have two magical winter towns. It behooves the mayor and me to try to help you guys out."

"She has a point," Misty said with a hint of disappointment in her voice.

"Honestly, guys, I think Rebecca is the intended target more than Silverlake," Megan continued.

"Funny you should say that because I've been thinking the same thing. Rebecca's been here before, and she has a history with the campground. I went out there today to talk with a former friend, and he pretty much dismissed me on the spot."

"Okay, that's something. I have a friend that works at WNN. She had a lot to stay. Not surprisingly, Rebecca stabbed people in the back and blamed them whenever things went south. She never took responsibility. One is her ex-producer," Megan continued.

"What does she look like?" For a moment, I thought that the ex-producer might be our mystery woman who I had seen around town.

"She is a he. Rebecca got him fired, and the man has been MIA ever since. I asked my friend to send me a picture of him and any coworkers who hated her to see if any of them look familiar."

"Maybe they've been hanging around town, and we just don't know who to look for," Misty added.

"Will you share the pictures with us when you get them?" I asked Megan.

"Absolutely. And will you guys share your information with me? I'd love nothing more than to bring some publicity to the Yuletide Times and get more people thinking about Mount Holly."

I reached my hand across the table. "It's a deal." And then we shook on it.

NINE

Later that night, I found myself hanging out in the lobby, waiting for Aunt Thelma to come back. I know I said I wasn't going to wait up for her, but I also said I wasn't going to let her out of my sight.

I glanced down at my phone. It was a little after nine o'clock. Still early.

Aunt Thelma could be anywhere doing a million different things, and it was none of my business. I reminded myself yet again that my aunt was a strong and powerful witch, and she could hold her own if it came down to it.

Not that I thought it would.

Truly, I agreed with Megan. Mayor Kringle looked smitten with my aunt. His motives could be altruistic, but that didn't mean I wouldn't keep my eye on him to be safe. Which meant I'd be hanging out in the lobby until Aunt Thelma came back.

Not only that, but Percy looked bored. And when Percy got bored, he got in trouble. The poltergeist stood hunched over the front desk. He rested one hand on his cheek with his elbow propped up on the countertop. He balled up little bits of paper with his other hand. The pile of paper balls was alarmingly impressive. Unless I wanted to scrap spitballs off the ceiling, Percy needed to find something else to do, fast.

"Go on. Get out of here," I said as I took up his post behind the counter.

"Really? You mean it?" Percy stood in a flash.

"Shoo," I motioned with my hand for him to leave. "I'm sure you can find something to do, like build a snowman." I grabbed the small trash can from under the counter and swiped the bits of paper into it.

"Outside people's windows to scare them?" Percy smiled mischievously.

"No. You'll give someone a heart attack." I shuddered. That would almost be as bad as the time the scarecrows came alive. Thank goodness we lived on the third floor, or I'm sure Percy would have already built a snowman outside my window.

"How about I hide in a snowman and jump out as people walk by?

"Also, no. No pranks."

"I got it!" Percy snapped his fingers. "I can peg unsuspecting tourists with snowballs!"

"Percy! You can not do that. Do you hear me? Percy? Percy!" But the poltergeist had already vanished. Where was his girlfriend, Eleanor when I needed her? She could usually keep him in line.

Megan and Cameron looked over at me from their post by the fire.

"Sorry. Poltergeist problems," I explained.

Megan nodded as if she dealt with ghosts on the regular. Cameron looked more unsure but went back to cleaning his camera or whatever he was doing to the lens.

I strolled over to Megan. She'd been typing away on her computer.

"Any word on those photos yet?" I asked.

Megan continued typing. "Not yet. Hopefully, I'll get them tomorrow." She stopped typing and looked over at me. "I'm running a background check on Michael. His last name is Strato, right?"

I nodded. I couldn't believe I hadn't thought to do that. Vance was usually pretty good at running background checks as needed.

"It looks like he has a prior record. An assault

charge and a restraining order against an Olivia Wade up in Atlanta."

I leaned down to read where Megan was pointing on her screen. "Yeah, that's him. Can you get any more details?"

"Let me see what I can do."

Cameron watched us with open curiosity. He had a soft cloth in one hand and a handheld camera balancing on his thigh.

"How about you? Are you doing okay?" I asked the cameraman.

"Huh?" Cameron snapped out of it. "What? Yeah, I'm doing okay. Sorry, just daydreaming."

"That's a nice camera. That's not the network's, is it?" It looked too small.

"This? No. This one's all mine." Cameron held it up and peered through the viewfinder. "I use it for documentaries. The size is more convenient.

"I didn't know you were a filmmaker," Megan remarked from her armchair.

"Trying to be, anyway. I haven't completed any projects yet."

"That's cool. What do you shoot."

"People, mostly. I like to tell stories." Cameron shrugged.

I nodded but didn't press Cameron for details. He didn't seem like he wanted to talk about it.

"Must be better than dealing with the likes of Rebecca," Megan remarked.

Cameron gave a nervous laugh. "I like working with Stormy, though, and the network offered hazard pay to stay." Cameron shrugged as if to say it wasn't all that bad.

I glanced over at the front door as Aunt Thelma came waltzing in with a broad smile on her face.

"Excuse me," I said to the duo and met my aunt upfront. She didn't quit walking until she was in the back office.

"Now, that was a date." Aunt Thelma removed her coat and hung it on the coat rack. "Such a gentleman too. It's a shame he lives all the way up in Mount Holly." Aunt Thelma pouted her lips while she thought. "Not sure if I want to try the whole long-distance dating thing. It never works out, does it?" Aunt Thelma's enthusiasm faltered.

"I don't know. Don't people always say absence makes the heart grow fonder?"

"Well, I suppose."

"And, if the roles were reversed, want to know what you'd say?"

Aunt Thelma quit fussing and turned her attention toward me. "You'd say don't throw a relationship away until you give it a chance."

"I would say that, wouldn't I?"

"I'm pretty sure you have said it. I take it you like him then? Wait, don't answer. It's written all over your face."

"I do. He's a very nice man. He's funny too, and you can't discredit humor. Heaven knows it's key to a happy life."

"This is true. Did he say anything about the curse or have any ideas who might be behind it?"

"You know, it didn't come up."

I shook my head. "What do you mean it didn't come up? How could it not?"

"I guess you had to be there." Aunt Thelma smiled once more.

I sighed.

"For what it's worth, I don't think he's your man," Aunt Thelma said on her way out of the room.

"No, I don't think he is either," I replied to the empty room.

My phone rang from somewhere beside me and shot me out of bed from a dead sleep. It was never a good thing when someone called you in the middle of the night.

Realizing it was my phone that had woken me, I began to search my comforter but came up empty.

All I found was an extra pillow and a wayward pair of socks. It would help if I turned on a light.

I twisted the switch of my bedside lamp and bathed the room in a soft glow. But it wasn't until I billowed the top sheet that I heard my phone hit the floor with a thud.

I dashed around the side of the bed and scooped it up.

"What's wrong?"

"I know it's late, and I'm sorry for calling, but I'm freaking out." The words rushed out of Misty's mouth in a single breath.

"What happened?"

"Daniel just left."

"Are you okay?"

"No. Yes. I don't know."

I knew I'd just woken up, but I wasn't following. "Misty, you're not making any sense."

Misty growled on the other end in frustration. "I know I'm not, and it's not like me!"

I squinted at my alarm clock. It was quarter after three in the morning. "Daniel just left?"

"I told you we spend hours talking. He loves to talk, and to dream, and to explore his feelings. Are you listening to me? A man who wants to talk about feelings." I could picture Misty shuddering on the other end of the line. Misty did not talk about her feelings. After realizing no one's life was in danger, I plopped back down in bed and tucked the covers around me.

"I've never had a man care about how I felt before. Truly cared about what I wanted, and not just for dinner but for the future. He wants a future with me," Misty continued.

"He said that?"

"Yes. I'm not sure what to think. I was just dating Peter. We had fun together, but I didn't fall for him. And, I might be falling for Daniel, or maybe I've already fallen. I can't be sure. How do you know? How does anyone know? I don't know what to think. I don't know what to feel, and I don't like it." Misty had done a fine job of working herself up.

"Take a deep breath. Calm down. It's going to be okay."

"How do you know it's going to be okay? Because from where I'm standing, the world's slipped off its axis, and I'm holding on for dear life."

I snickered on the other line.

"Are you laughing at me? This is not funny! I am Misty McQuaid. I don't get weak in the knees over a man, I don't talk about feelings, and I certainly don't fall in love."

"You realize you sound ridiculous right now."

"That's what you lead with? That I sound ridiculous? I'm having an existential crisis here!"

I tried not to laugh again. I buried the phone into my chest and took a calming breath in through my nose and out through my mouth to regain my composure. Misty was right. This was not like her at all. But to be honest, it was the best thing that could happen to her. Misty was always so sure of everything. She always knew what she wanted, where she was going, and how she would get there until Daniel came along. Sometimes the unexpected moments in life turned out to be the most rewarding.

"Hello? Are you there?" Misty said when I put the phone back up to my ear.

"Yes, sorry. I'm here."

"What am I going to do?"

"I don't think you have to do anything."

"What do you mean?"

"Well, what did Daniel say exactly? Did he ask you to marry him?"

"What? Gosh, no. He just asked if I wanted to go on tour."

"That's it?" I closed my eyes and shook my head.

"It's cross country! I'd be gone for weeks. Practically the entire summer if I stayed the whole time."

"Do you want to go on tour?"

"I don't know. Yes? It sounds like fun, but I have a business to run. I can't up and leave town."

"True, but you also have Vicki. She could run the shop for a week or two. I could help out too."

"You'd do that?"

"Of course. I think it would be good for you to spend some time with Daniel."

"He said it's pretty boring," Misty said. "A lot of driving and time sitting around doing nothing." Even though Misty described a dull situation, I could tell she still wanted to go. She just needed to give herself permission.

"If I were you, I'd go."

"You would?"

"Uh-huh. I'd talk to Vicki, see what weeks work best, and then fly out and meet Daniel wherever he's at."

"I suppose I could do that."

"Take it from someone who knows—If you think you might love Daniel, or you could one day love him, then you owe it to yourself to give it a shot."

Misty was silent on the other end. "When did you get so smart in the relationship department?"

"When my best friend made me realize how much I still cared for Vance."

"I did help you remember that didn't I?"

"You were brutal. It's only fair that I return the favor."

"Consider it returned. I'm going to call Daniel right now."

"Right now?"

"Why not? He's a rockstar. He never sleeps."

I yawned into the phone. "Well, this witch does. Talk to you tomorrow?"

"Talk to you tomorrow. Night."

"Good night." I clicked off with Misty and, surprisingly, was able to drift back off to sleep.

TEN

The next morning, I got up bright and early. I planned to interview Gertie and see if Michael had an alibi for New Year's Eve. Maybe I could also find out how he was acting leading up to it.

I also wanted to try and identify the mystery woman. If Michael wasn't the bad guy, maybe she was. Find the mystery woman, case closed. If only it were that simple.

I shot a text off to Clemmie to make sure we were still on for two o'clock. The woman must've had her phone right beside her because she replied seconds later that she would be ready to roll. Those were her exact words. Clemmie even included a smiley face emoji wearing sunglasses with the text.

But before I could do any sleuthing, I had to

work the front desk for a few hours. The snow was relentless through the night, and I agreed with Aunt Thelma when she called all off-site help off for the day. That left me, Aunt Thelma, and Percy to hold down the fort. After a quick bite of breakfast, I headed downstairs to get to work. However, my plans took a detour.

As I passed the second-floor foyer, I knew something was wrong. My first instinct was that the thermostat had broken, and the heat turned off sometime in the middle of the night. But then I noticed the snow. Big, thick flakes fell from the ceiling.

"Percy? Is this your idea of a joke?" I had no idea how the poltergeist could make it snow, but if there were a way, he would've discovered it. I shivered and tucked my hands in my jeans pocket. I would need more than just a sweater to tackle this problem. I was stuck deciding what to do. Should I run upstairs and grab my coat? Or should I go downstairs and talk with Percy and see if he was really behind this.

That's when I noticed ice around the door of Room 214.

My stomach immediately sank. It was Paige's room.

I debated for a split second if I should enter the room or not, and then common sense kicked in, and I decided to call Deputy Jones instead.

"Jones here," the deputy said when he picked up the transferred call.

"Hey, Deputy Jones, it's Angelica."

"Like I told Vance, we're still in the preliminary stages of this investigation."

"No, it's not that. It's snowing on the second floor of the inn."

"Come again?"

"You heard me right. It's snowing inside Mystic Inn. I have clouds hanging from the ceiling and snow piling up on the second floor. Not only that but there's ice surrounding room 214. It's Paige's room."

Deputy Jones didn't miss a beat.

"Don't do anything. You hear me?"

"Loud and clear. Don't worry. I have no intention of opening that door." I might be curious as to what had happened inside, but I wasn't about to unleash a blizzard inside the hotel.

"The sheriff and I are on our way."

I wasn't necessarily happy to know Deputy Jones was bringing the sheriff, but I wasn't sure what else I expected. Of course, the sheriff would want to know about this.

I hung up with the deputy and then went downstairs to break the news to my aunt and call Vance.

"What now?" Vance sounded a lot like Deputy Jones when I tried to explain to him what had happened. Vance had gone in to work to get caught up on some paperwork when I had reached him.

"I know. It's crazy, isn't it?"

"Is Paige inside?"

"Ah, I have no idea. I hadn't even thought of it. I don't know why." Suddenly, something that had seemed bizarre turned heartbreaking. "Vance, this is bad." I liked Paige, truly. What if the same fate that befell her sister had hit her too? I started to feel sick to my stomach.

"I'm on my way," was the last thing Vance said before hanging up the phone.

"Now, what do we do?" Aunt Thelma asked me.

"How many extra rooms do we have?" Most of our guests should be checking out soon since a majority of the reservations were through Sunday only.

"I'm not sure. Let me check." Aunt Thelma began clicking through the computer system.

"Let's see if we have enough rooms to bump everyone off the second floor. That way, we can section off that corridor and try to keep the first floor warm and toasty.

"Which one of you guys made it snow upstairs?" Percy asked as he walked through the kitchenette wall into the lobby.

"It wasn't one of us, trust me. I was hoping it was you," I confessed.

"No, but that's a great idea. How would I make that work?" Percy pretended to stroke his invisible beard.

"Don't you dare." Aunt Thelma rarely raised her voice to Percy, so you can bet that when she did, she meant business.

Percy held up his hands in surrender. "Don't worry, boss. I promise I'll stay out of it." Aunt Thelma replied with a head nod to let Percy know she had heard him.

Vance arrived on the scene at the same time Deputy Jones and Sheriff Reynolds did.

"Which way to the room?" Sheriff Reynolds said by way of greeting.

"This way," I motioned for the gentlemen to follow me. This time I was prepared. I tugged my mittens back on and then jammed my arms in my coat sleeves and buttoned it up. "It's cold up there," I said to no one in particular. Aunt Thelma threw on her coat, and together we trudged up the stairs.

Once we reached the room, I dug in my jeans pocket for the room key. The only problem was the card reader was frozen over. There was no way to stick the card in to unlock the door.

"Stand back," Sheriff Reynolds said, drawing his wand.

"What are you going to do exactly?" Aunt Thelma said with alarm. I was thinking the same thing. The snow, and consequently the water damage, would be bad enough. I didn't need the sheriff blasting a hole in the wall too.

The sheriff ignored us and instead replied, "Cover your ears!"

Aunt Thelma did one better. "Muffalo!" she quickly commanded, placing a protective bubble around us.

In the next second, a sonic boom filled the hallway. Instinctively, I clamped my mittened hands over my ears and flinched even though the sound didn't reach us. The vibrating sound waves rippled the bubble that surrounded us, but Aunt Thelma's ward held. The force shattered the ice covering the door.

Sheriff Reynolds turned around and stared at us with his hand extended, waiting for me to hand him the card. Aunt Thelma popped the bubble, and I passed the room key over.

"Wait," Aunt Thelma moved forward. "I don't want whatever's going on in that room spilling into this hallway any more than it already has. I'm putting a sealing charm on the door so that way it all stays put."

"All right then. Not a bad idea," the sheriff agreed. He stepped aside and allowed my aunt to work her magic.

I didn't even know what a sealing charm was, but I soon found out as a transparent film covered the outside of the door. It looked like a giant sheet of plastic wrap. "This should help keep whatever's in there at bay," Aunt Thelma commented to me.

It was a good thing one of us had the skills and forethought because as soon as the sheriff opened the door, a gust of wind blew out, hitting the film and making it balloon. Inside the room, it was like the scene at Wishing Well Park, only worse. Snow was waist-high. If you didn't know the room's layout, you'd have no idea where the bed, end tables, or dresser was. I craned my neck. Aunt Thelma seemed afraid to look.

"This is going to call for some old fashion equipment," Deputy Jones remarked. "Do you have a shovel?"

I nodded.

"I'll go get it," Vance volunteered.

Within a few moments, Deputy Jones had cleared a path through the hotel room. When they reached the bathroom, it was like nothing I'd ever seen before. The door was stuck from the inside due to a mixture of ice and snow. Deputy Jones used the blunt end of the shovel to chip away at the ice, eventually allowing the door to pull free and swing freely inward.

I was shocked at the sight. There was another life-sized ice sculpture.

"Is that Paige?" Vance whispered from beside me.

"No! Not another person," Aunt Thelma's eyes crinkled with worry.

"I don't know. I can't tell." I swallowed uncomfortably.

Deputy Jones made his way back to us. "I think you need to see this."

"Is that Paige?" I asked without moving.

"No, I don't know who she is. I'm hoping you do."

"It's not Paige? But this is her room, I'm sure of it." It didn't make sense.

Deputy Jones motioned for me to follow him.

"We'll stay out here, dear." Aunt Thelma tugged her coat tighter around her neck with her gloved hand. Vance sent me a reassuring smile.

I nodded to them both.

The moment we crossed the threshold, the bitter coldness of the room hit me in the face. It was like being doused in a bucket of ice water. It was the type of cold that went bone-deep. I wasn't staying in that room a second longer than was absolutely necessary.

"Do you know who she is?" The sheriff asked us as we came closer.

It took me a second to find my voice, because yes, I did know who it was.

It was Megan.

I nodded. "She's a reporter for the Yuletide Times. Her name's Megan Mulroney, but I have no idea what she's doing in here." My teeth began to chatter. I wasn't the only one freezing. Sheriff Reynold's nose was bright red, and Deputy Jones had his hands stuffed in his pockets and his shoulders hunched close to his ears.

"How about we continue this conversation downstairs," the sheriff said after reading the room.

Now that, I could agree with.

Our group reconvened downstairs in the back office. None of us chose to sit. Instead, the five of us stood about the room—Aunt Thelma and I behind the large oak desk with Vance leaning behind the back side table. Deputy Jones stood by the door while the sheriff stood across from my aunt and me.

"How well do you know this Paige woman?" The sheriff looked to both my aunt and me to answer.

"I don't know her much at all. Angelica, you've talked with her a time or two, haven't you?"

"Yeah, we talked once or twice. She seems like a nice person."

"When's the last time you saw her?" The sheriff asked.

I had to think for a moment. "I think it was New Year's Eve." I looked behind me to Vance. He nodded his head in confirmation. "Vance and I were working the front desk when Deputy Jones dropped her off shortly after 2 AM."

The sheriff looked back at his deputy. "Is that true? Did you give the woman a lift?"

Deputy Jones nodded. "I did. With the way the snow was coming down, I didn't think it was right to send the woman off on her own in the middle of the night. I dropped her off here just like they said." Deputy Jones nodded toward Vance and me.

"And that's the last time you saw her or spoke with her?"

"Yes?" It had been a busy 36 hours since then, but I couldn't recall seeing Paige after that.

"Okay, if you see her, call the station right away." The sheriff turned to Deputy Jones. "Let's get eyes out looking for her. We need to bring her in for questioning, stat."

"You got it boss."

I interrupted the sheriff. "You don't think Paige froze Megan, do you?"

"Did you give out any extra room keys? Does anyone else have access to Paige's room?"

"No. I didn't give out any extra keys, did you, Aunt Thelma?"

"Oh no, dear. Paige only requested one room key."

"Unless you're telling me that you or your aunt broke in Paige's room and set off a winter bomb, who else am I supposed to suspect?" The sheriff gave me a pitying stare. "Looks like your crime-solving skills are slipping a bit. I always knew it was more luck than brains that got you this far."

I glared back at the sheriff but kept my mouth shut. "Let's go, Jones. We got work to do."

The two men left the office in short order.

"Well then," Aunt Thelma fidgeted with the pearl necklace that she wore. "I don't know what to think."

"I don't know either," I confessed.

"I hate to admit it, but the sheriff has a point. You said so yourself. Rebecca was mean to her sister. For all we know, Megan figured it out, and she went to confront Paige and POW!"

"But wouldn't she be hit with it too?" I asked.

"I don't know, not if it was her spell. She might know how to deflect it," Vance pointed out.

Aunt Thelma sighed. "This is a sad turn of events."

I agreed.

"I guess we should get the word out that we need to find Paige."

"Do you think she's still in town?" Vance asked.

"If I were Paige, I would be long gone by now," Aunt Thelma remarked.

"Me too, but that doesn't mean we can't at least give people a heads up. Maybe someone saw her this morning." I assume that's when the winter bomb went off. A guest would've reported snowing on the second floor earlier if it had happened last night.

"I'll give Clemmie a call," Aunt Thelma said.

"I'll call Misty at the bookstore and have her tell Vicki too.

"Let me give Luke a call," Vance said.

"Good point. I feel bad. He and Paige hit it off. If anyone has seen her recently, it's probably him." I pointed out.

Vance and I walked out of the back office to keep an eye on the front. I had just gotten ahold of Misty and told her what was happening when the person in question walked right up the back deck and into the lobby. Paige and Luke were laughing and smiling, bundled up in winter gear. Luke had a pair of ice skates slung over his shoulder while Paige's skates dangled by their laces from her hand.

I was speechless.

"What? What's happened?" Luke said when he took in my appearance. Paige's face immediately fell. The two walked forward, and I noticed that Luke didn't let go of her hand.

"Er?" I turned to Vance to help me out. I wasn't sure what to say.

Vance came right out with it. "The sheriff was just here. He's looking for Paige."

"The sheriff? What's wrong. Is my sister okay? This is what I get for having fun. I knew I shouldn't have left my room."

"And what time did you leave your room?" Vance and I eyed Paige, eager for her answer.

Paige looked over at Luke before answering. "We met for breakfast a little after eight down at the diner."

"And then I convinced Paige to go ice-skating with me. Will someone tell us what's going on?" Luke's eyes darted between Vance and me, waiting for an explanation.

I doubted the sheriff wanted us to say anything, but it looked like Paige had an alibi, and if that was the case, she wasn't the bad guy. Then again, if the incident happened before eight o'clock, Paige could be responsible, and if we broke the news to her, we could see her reaction and be the judge.

With my mind made up, I decided to spill the beans. "There was an attack. Someone unleashed the winter spell again. This time it was in Paige's room, and it got Megan."

"Megan?" Paige looked bewildered. She retracted her neck and looked to Luke for clarification. It was clear Paige didn't know who I was talking about.

"She's a reporter for the Yuletide times. She's staying here as a guest."

"What was she doing in my room, and who set off the bomb?" Paige asked.

"That's what we're trying to figure out," Vance replied.

Aunt Thelma rushed out from the back office. "Okay, Clemmie's on the lookout. I told her to call me if she sees Paige." My aunt realized Paige was standing in front of her at that moment. "Oh. Never mind then."

Paige looked horror-struck. "The sheriff thinks it's me? That's why he wants to talk to me?" The ice skates fell to the floor with a clunk.

"It was the general thought," I confessed with a sheepish expression.

"But why? I would never do such a thing. I can't

believe this is happening." Paige dropped Luke's hand and used it to cover her eyes as she choked back sobs.

Luke lowered his skates and brought Paige in for an embrace. She dropped her hand and buried her face into his shoulder instead.

"Well. Now I feel bad," Aunt Thelma remarked at the emotional scene.

I turned away. "I know, me too."

"Regardless of how we feel, the logic's still there. The bad guy caught Megan and then used the spell to getaway. That's what makes the most sense."

"Again, the million-dollar question is, who is that someone?"

"And why is it happening right under our noses?" Aunt Thelma added.

"We've never needed security cameras in the hallways before, but maybe it's something we should think about." Mystic Inn was our home, and I didn't like the idea of having cameras everywhere, but this needed to stop. We had to solve this case.

Luke motioned with his head above Paige's. "You guys need to figure out what's going on here. This is getting out of control."

"I know," I said on an exhale.

Paige stepped away from Luke and wiped away her eyes with her sleeve. "I promise I have nothing to do with any of this. I'll call the sheriff right now. I have nothing to hide. I'll even drink a truth serum if it comes down to it."

"It won't come to that." From the tone of Luke's voice, he wasn't going to allow it to come to that.

"Luke's right. I'm sure once you tell the sheriff where you've been, he'll realize you've been set up," I tried to reassure Paige.

"You're assuming Sheriff Reynolds is going to act rational," Vance said to me under his breath.

I turned away from Luke and Paige. "Well, yes, there is that," I acquiesced.

"You and I both know that the sheriff's going to want someone arrested and charged as soon as possible. It's the way he is."

"I agree, but it's doesn't do Paige any good to hide. It only makes her look guilty."

"No, but she needs to be smart."

Speaking of being smart. I turned around and faced Paige once more. Luke was still trying to reassure her. "We'll figure this out. Don't worry," he said.

Paige looked like she was trying to steel her resolve.

"I just thought of something. Did you let anyone in your room yesterday? Or give anyone else a key?" I thought that if there was a time curse involved, perhaps someone had planted it, and Megan just happened to be at the wrong place at the wrong time.

"No, I only have one room key. I was in and out yesterday, but no one was in my room." Paige seemed to think it through for a moment and then shrugged her shoulders. "I wish I had something helpful to say."

"It's not your fault that you don't. But someone did try breaking into The Candy Cauldron last night," Luke said.

"They what now?" Aunt Thelma spoke up for the first time.

"When I got in this morning, my wards were tripped."

"Did you report it to the sheriff?" Vance asked.

"I did. I thought maybe one of the deputies tripped them."

"Isn't someone guarding the freezer?" I asked.

"They were, but we figured with the extra wards, we didn't need to keep an overnight vigil," Vance replied.

"That makes sense," I replied.

Paige excused herself and walked across the lobby to retrieve a tissue. Luke leaned in as if imparting the secret. "And I have to be honest with you guys, having Mayor Parrish and Rebecca in the freezer is freaking me out. Every time I get a frozen batch of strawberries, it gives me the heebie-jeebies. They stand there just staring at me."

I grimaced because that would creep me out too.

"Okay, where she at," Deputy Amber said as she strolled into the lobby.

"Deputy Reynolds, how lovely to see you," Aunt Thelma said.

Paige had been walking back to join us when she faltered.

At that moment, Amber spotted her. "You! Freeze right there." She drew her wand and pointed it at Paige's chest.

"Poor choice of words, don't you think?" Luke's voice was deadly calm. He glared at Amber. His eyes flashed with anger. I'd never seen Luke so possessive before. I just hoped Paige wasn't clouding his judgment.

I planned to tell Amber that she had it all wrong, but Luke beat me to it. "Before you go around making accusations, you should know the facts. And the facts are that Paige was with me this morning. She wasn't anywhere near her room. And it's not like this is Fort Knox. Any witch with a wand could break into a hotel room. So go ahead and call the sheriff and tell him that you found Paige. But you should know that we were headed his way anyway, and we'll be bringing our lawyer." Luke motioned to Vance. "That okay with you?"

"Is that okay with you?" Vance directed his question to Paige.

Paige nodded yes. A loose tear slipped down her cheek. She used her knuckle to brush it away.

"Excellent, just the people I wanted to see." Six heads swiveled in Stormy Evans's direction. "Which one of you wants to give me an exclusive?"

Amber readily stepped forward. "That would be me. What would you like to know?" Amber tugged down the front of her coat and strutted over to Stormy like she was a boss.

"You, don't move," she shot over her shoulder at Paige.

Paige flinched.

"Don't worry. She tells me the same thing all the time," I remarked.

"Me too, dear," Aunt Thelma agreed.

Paige replied with a weak smile.

Stormy managed to coax Amber in front of the fireplace for the interview.

Paige frowned as the scene unfolded.

"Let Amber talk to her," Vance remarked.

"I know, but who knows what she's going to say about me?" Paige replied.

"She's not going to say much if she values her

job," Luke practically growled. I didn't doubt that Luke meant every word and that Vance would be willing to take up the case if Amber slandered Paige's name.

I turned to Vance. "While you're gone, I'm going to see about getting everyone transferred off the second floor. Maybe Percy can help with the snow removal, and then I'll be at that Simmering Sisters meeting. I'll catch up with you a little bit?"

"Alright. Let me know what you find out."

"You too."

oretta Johnson lived in a neat and tidy red-brick home down the street from the high school. Even though snow continued to fall, Loretta's driveway was completely snow-free. And unlike her neighbors, Loretta had put away all her holiday decor and somehow found the time to switch it out for spring already. As we walked up to the porch, a sign with the words *Welcome Spring* scrolled on it greeted us. The cheery wooden sign hung in place where her holiday wreath previously stood just yesterday.

"I forgot to ask. What did you make?" I looked over at Clemmie. She carried a white ceramic casserole dish with a glass lid. I tried to peer inside, but the glass fogged over.

"Make? I didn't make anything. I picked up some

scalloped potatoes from The Grove and sprinkled a little parsley on top. As long as you don't say anything, no one will ever know." Clemmie kept her voice low.

"Well, this is a surprise," Loretta said when she answered the door and took in my appearance. From the tone of her voice, I could tell it wasn't a pleasant surprise.

"Loretta, you know Angelica. She's a wonderful cook. You should be honored if she joined your club here." Clemmie hooked her thumb in my direction.

I tried to keep a straight face. I was not a wonderful cook. I mean, I knew my way around the kitchen, but I couldn't tell you the last time I made a meal worth mentioning. I raised my eyebrows in response, trying to look pleased with Clemmie's praise.

Loretta seemed to assess me in a new light. "Is that so? And what did you make for us today?"

"Oh, I didn't make—" I started to say.

Clemmie thrust the casserole dish out to Loretta. "Her famous scalloped potatoes. You have to try them. They're the best."

I cleared my throat.

"Is that so?" Loretta looked down at the dish.

"Angelica, is that you?" Mrs. Potts said as she came up behind Loretta.

"Hello." I waved at my former teacher.

"Well, are you going to let them in or make them stand outside in the snow all afternoon?" Mrs. Potts glared at Loretta.

"Yes, of course. Where are my manners?" Loretta glared back at Mrs. Potts.

"Angelica, I didn't know you liked to cook. You never said anything."

I was about to whisper to Mrs. Potts that I didn't, when Clemmie spoke up.

"She's just full of hidden talents. Now, what do we have good to eat?"

I kept my mouth shut.

I'm not saying Loretta was a neat freak, but she had white carpeting in her kitchen. What kind of psycho has white carpeting in their kitchen? It's just as bad as people who carpet their bathrooms. Do they not ever spill anything?

"Let's see what y'all got today," Clemmie said as she scoped out the buffet laid out on the side table.

Mrs. Potts sidled up to me and looped her arm through mine. "If you love to bake, then I insist you try my peach cobbler. I canned the peaches myself this summer and sprinkled little extra sunshine in them. It feels like summer with every bite."

Loretta Johnson heard the exchange. "Any southern witch can throw together a cobbler. But you have to have skills to pull off a pecan pie." Loretta motioned to the classic, rich dessert at the end of the table. "I picked the nuts myself from Wishing Well Park."

Mrs. Potts snorted. It was the most unladylike sound I'd ever heard her make. "You did not. I saw you buy two bags of pecans at the market last week."

Loretta put her hand on her hip and stared down Mrs. Potts. "Are you calling me a liar?"

"Liar, cheat, teller of untruths. Whatever you want to call it, you are a big fat fibber."

"I most certainly am not!" Loretta stood with her back ramrod straight and an indignant expression on her face.

Gertie came out of the guest bathroom, drying her hands off on a towel. I was relieved to see her. Hopefully, I'd get a chance to ask her about Michael and Rebecca. "Don't let her act fool you. Loretta's full of nonsense, but I bet her pie isn't half bad." Gertie winked at me as she passed by. I quickly realized that Gertie was a no-nonsense kind of woman. She kept her gray hair short, and she wore jeans and a red flannel shirt. Unlike Loretta with her fancy hair clip, flowery blouse and cream-colored slacks.

Speaking of Loretta, she looked unsure of how to take the backhand compliment.

"I'd love to try both," I interjected before Loretta could come back with a biting retort.

"But try the cobbler first," Mrs. Potts put in under her breath.

"What are you whispering over there?" Loretta eyed Mrs. Potts suspiciously.

"None of your business, that's what," Mrs. Potts shot back before turning to me. "I'm sorry. That woman grinds my gears. I wish it wasn't so." I'd known Mrs. Potts didn't care for Loretta too much, but this was the first time I had witnessed the all-out hostility firsthand. However, Mrs. Potts needn't apologize. I knew first-hand how it felt to have someone get under your skin.

"Heard you had a bit of excitement over at your place this morning," Gertie said as I sat beside her with a scoop of cobbler and a slice of pie.

"What's happened now?" Loretta walked around offering tea or coffee while club members continued to arrive. "Coffee?" she stopped in front of me.

"Yes, please." I turned over my cup, and dabbed the corner of my mouth with my napkin.

"A guest got the deep freeze," Clemmie replied knowingly.

A gasp echoed through the dining room.

"No! How awful," Loretta paused mid-pour.

"Who was it?" Mrs. Potts asked.

"A reporter from Mount Holly," Clemmie replied without missing a beat.

"And you don't know who did it?" asked Carol Keyes, the retired librarian. I didn't even know she'd arrived.

"Not a clue," Clemmie continued before I could get a word in.

"I don't like this at all. What if one of us is next? I live alone." Carol looked around the group.

I finally had a moment to speak up. "I wouldn't worry too much. I think Rebecca was the intended target, and Megan, that's the reporter, got too close to uncovering the truth."

"What about Mayor Parrish then?" Loretta looked skeptical.

I thought for a second. "A case of being at the wrong place at the wrong time. Mayor Parrish wasn't supposed to be on stage when the ball dropped."

"She wasn't?" All five ladies said in unison.

I shook my head. "I overheard Rebecca talking with the cameraman when they decided to do another interview. It was last minute."

"Sounds like a premeditated freezing to me," Clemmie remarked.

"Me too," I agreed.

Just then, a couple of other club members arrived, and the topic of conversation shifted. Soon the women were talking about plans for a spring cookbook and bake sale. This year's fundraiser was to raise money for Witches End Hunger. A nonprofit that tackled food scarcity in the supernatural community.

It would be almost an hour before I was able to talk with Gertie again.

"Hey, I wanted to ask you about something," I said to Gertie after the meeting wrapped up and everyone was busy having side conversations.

"What's that now?"

"I heard Rebecca used to work at the campground."

"Work's a pretty generous word."

"I heard that as well."

"Then you also heard we told her not to come back."

I nodded. "But while she was here, her and Michael became friends."

"There you go again, being generous with your definitions," Gertie replied.

"What was it then?"

"A summer fling I suppose. Nothing serious."

I looked unsure.

"Now I know what you're thinking. Sure, those two have history, but they haven't seen each other for years."

"Yes, they have. The night before New Year's Eve at the tavern," Clemmie joined the conversation. I had no idea she was even listening in. Clemmie was sneaky like that.

I turned to Clemmie. "Why am I just now hearing about this?"

"I forgot about it, that's all. Gertie just jogged my memory."

"Do you know what they talked about?" I asked.

"Oh, you know Rebecca. She was bragging about her success and how famous she is now and he's still a big, fat nobody. Michael didn't like that."

"Michael isn't a nobody. And this conversation is pointless. He wouldn't do anything to her. This winter spell has been awful for business, and Michael works so hard at the campground." Gertie jumped to her grandson's defense.

I wasn't too sure. Didn't they say revenge was best served cold? And I couldn't forget about Michael's assault charge. I bet Gertie didn't know about it. Or if she did, she wouldn't admit to it.

"Any idea where Michael was New Year's Eve?" I asked gently.

"Wherever he was, I doubt he was breaking the law." Gertie glared at me.

The ladies' side conversations died down and once again they were focused on the case.

"It would help if we knew what kind of spell was used," Mrs. Potts muttered.

"Well, my money is on a time curse. Enchant an object, set a clock, and ta-da, you have a curse just waiting to go off."

"I don't know about that." Mrs. Potts seemed to think Loretta's theory was ridiculous. "My money's on a potion. That ball had to weigh at least a hundred pounds. Set a potion underneath it, and the moment that ball crashes it? POW! Instant winter."

"And how is that any different from my time curse idea?"

"It's completely different. It's a curse versus a potion. The mechanics aren't even remotely the same," Mrs. Potts replied.

While the two ladies continued to go back and forth, I remembered the piece of glass that I had found on the ground. Could it have been used to house the potion? I wasn't about to throw my thoughts into the mix and bring up the glass, but I decided then and there I would make a stop at Connie's potion shop as soon as the meeting was over.

After dropping Clemmie off at home, I headed to the potion shop and, like before, Village Square was almost deserted. The snow-covered roads had become ice-covered, making it difficult to safely drive. I crossed my fingers that the worst of the winter bomb was behind us. It was impossible to make out the lines on the road. You had to trust you were in the right lane and not yarding the neighbors. It would take some time before people could drive smoothly around town again.

Bonnie from the tavern was out front, deicing her sidewalk with a fire charm when I passed by.

"You make that look easy," I replied with a smile.

"Grew up in Minnesota," Bonnie replied with a throaty laugh.

I carefully watched my step as I navigated the cobblestone path to Mix it Up! I loved stopping by the potions shop because you never knew what you would find, not to mention the smells. Some days the shop smelled sweet like cotton candy as a pink, glittery haze drifted down the aisles. Other days, it smelled like death, and you'd have to hold your breath or use a bubble charm to keep from gagging.

Connie was almost always brewing up some new concoction, and today was no exception. The potion master was at her usual post behind the counter when I walked through the door. A purple flame licked the bottom of her copper cauldron as Connie stood before it, using her wand to stir the air above the pot. Connie's lips moved as she recited a spell. I stood in the entryway, careful not to break her focus.

In the next instant, a jet of thick, gray smoke shot out of the cauldron and gathered above Connie's head.

Startled, I jumped back. My back scraped against the handle of the shop's glass front door.

"Gah!" Connie dashed aside and reached for an umbrella. The fact it was readily on hand, told me this wasn't the first time it had happened. A dark cloud churned angrily in the air, and rain began to pour down. A low rumble soon followed. Connie began to frantically search for her wand, which she'd dropped when reaching for the umbrella. It was then that she spotted me.

"Give me a minute," she hollered over the continuing thunder overhead. "I'll get this cleared up in no time."

Connie plucked up her wand from the linoleum and pointed it at the offending apparition. With a flick of her wrist and another incantation, the cloud quickly vanished. All that remained was a puddle on the floor.

"Here, let me help." I stepped forward and eyed the area, looking for a towel.

Connie dipped her head below the counter and plopped a roll of paper towel on top. "Thank you, I appreciate it." Connie then turned and grabbed the mop propped up in the corner and made quick work of the puddle.

It was amazing. The entire store smelled like petrichor—that earthy aroma I associated with springtime after a rainstorm—which was crazy because there wasn't any damp earth here, only wet vinyl flooring.

"Now, that that's cleaned up, what can I do for you?"

"First off, I need that spell." I pointed at the ceiling where the cloud had been. "I have a snow cloud on the second floor that I don't know how to get rid of."

"Oh, no problem. It's pretty simple. I'll write it down for you." Connie got out a piece of paper and started writing down her spell on it. "Magic gone wrong?" That was Connie's polite way of asking if it was my fault. My wayward spells were notorious in these parts.

"I wish. Someone let off another winter bomb in one of our rooms."

"No!" Connie stopped writing. "Was anyone hurt?"

I nodded solemnly. "A guest. Megan Mulroney. She's a reporter from Mount Holly."

"I'm sorry. I hadn't heard. How awful. I don't suppose you know who did it?"

"No. The spell went off in another guest room, and she claims she has no idea how it got there."

"Do you believe her?" Connie had returned to writing down the spell, but looked up when asking the question.

I sighed. "Yes?" The word was a question, not a statement. "It's Paige, Rebecca's sister. Not sure if you know her."

"She stopped in," Connie confirmed.

I nodded. "She's devastated. Swears she has nothing to do with it and even offered to take a truth serum."

Connie raised her eyebrows.

"And she's formed a fast friendship with Luke, who swears she's innocent."

"Do you think she's bewitched him?"

"Gosh, I hope not. That almost seems worse than cursing her sister. At least her sister had it coming," I clarified.

"But?"

It was hard to miss the uneasiness in my voice. "But Paige makes the most sense. She had the means and the motive with how mean her sister was to her. I guess I don't know what to think."

"In the meantime, let's clean up that cloud for you." Connie handed over the slip of paper.

I read the spell. It seemed straightforward. "Anything special I need to do? Clap three times? Spin in a circle? Say a prayer to Mother Nature?"

Connie smiled. "No, saying the words should suffice."

I pocketed the note. "Okay, good deal. I also wanted to run something by you, and from the looks of it, you might be thinking the same thing as me."

"Go on." Connie greeted another guest as they entered her shop.

I kept my voice low.

"I was at a Simmering Sisters' meeting this afternoon, and Mrs. Potts said she believes the winter curse was a potion, and when the ball dropped, it broke a vial and released the spell. Here's the thing, I found glass at the base of the ball."

"You did not." Connie's eyes widened at the discovery.

"I did. I don't have it on me, but it's a shimmering blue glass. There's more stuck in the enchanted ice. I pointed it out to Amber, but she didn't think anything of it."

"Okay, my goodness. This is exactly what I was thinking." Connie clapped her hands together in excitement before settling back down. "So, get this, there are weather potions. You mix them up in a vial and shake it up. Then when you break them, it unleashes the storm. Or, that's how they work in theory. Weather spells are outside of my wheelhouse, but I've been experimenting. On a small scale, obviously." Connie motioned to the store. "But they're unstable. It's tricky magic. But, if I can figure out how to make them, then I can figure out how to reverse them."

"That's a brilliant idea."

"In theory. All I've managed to do so far is make it rain."

"Well, I have all the faith in the world that you'll figure this out."

"Thanks. But it still doesn't explain how to transform Mayor Parrish and Rebecca back."

"No, but it's a step in the right direction. Let me know if I can help in any way." Maybe I could hold the umbrella.

"Thanks. And let me know how the spell goes. I can stop by after close and help."

"It's okay. I'll give it a shot." How hard could it be?

TWELVE

I left Connie's with a copy of her spell in my pocket and a pep in my step. I was on a mission. I knew what I needed to do. First, I would try to disperse the snow cloud on the second floor. Then, I was going to search Paige's room for clues. The only problem was I knew the room was an active crime scene, and I would be in hot water if anyone caught me inside. But, if we were going to solve the case, we needed evidence. If we were right, and a potion was involved, maybe the vial was still in the hotel room, like at the park. If the culprit broke the glass to release the storm, then there should be fragments in the ice like at the base of the countdown ball. I'd think about how the potion came to be in Paige's room after the fact.

"You're back already, dear?" Aunt Thelma said

from behind the registration desk. A bouquet of long-stem red roses, complete with foliage and baby's breath, stood off to the side in a crystal-cut vase.

"From Mayor Kringle?" I motioned to the flowers.

"I told you he was a gentleman," Aunt Thelma replied nonchalantly, but only I could see the light pink coloring tinge her cheeks.

I changed the subject. "How's the second floor?"

Aunt Thelma shook her head. "Percy's been cleaning it up, but I'm sure we're going to have to replace the carpet. There's only so much water you can put on the floor before it ruins it. It's a darn shame the carpet was practically new." My aunt looked up at the ceiling as if waiting for water to start dripping down.

"Hopefully, it won't come to that. Connie gave me a weather spell to try."

Aunt Thelma twisted her lips. "A weather spell? Huh, never tried one of those before."

"I'm going to head up and see how it works."

Aunt Thelma didn't ask any questions because at that moment, she was interrupted by a new guest.

I purposely didn't tell Aunt Thelma my plan to sneak into Paige's room. That way, she couldn't be an accessory to the crime. Thankfully, we still had an extra copy of Paige's room key in the back office from earlier when the sheriff entered. I slipped into the office and retrieved the key from the drawer, and quickly pocketed it before strolling back out.

I waved goodbye to my aunt, who was still talking to the new guest, another reporter by the sounds of it, and took the stairs up to the second floor.

The moment I rounded the second-floor landing, it was like stepping into an arctic wonderland. I tugged my hat down firmly and pulled my collar up around my neck, and then I spotted Percy.

"What in the world are you doing?" I asked the poltergeist. Instead of cleaning up the snow, Percy had been playing with it. He had created a whole family of snowmen, marching right down the hall in a single file line.

"Meet Mr. Jangles, his wife Mary Jangles, and their kids, Bobby, Tommy, Sally, and Susie."

I slapped my hand over my face. "You cannot build a snowman family on the second floor. We need to clean this up right away."

"I've been cleaning this up all day, and it keeps on snowing. I think it's about time we had a little bit of fun."

"You can build a snowman outside. I promise. I'll even help. But first, we need to get rid of these guys."

"Cover your ears, kids. Don't listen to her!" Percy shouted to the make-believe family.

I glared in response.

"Fine, fine. But how are we supposed to do that? It's been snowing up here all morning."

I cleared my throat and removed my wand from my coat pocket. "Connie gave me a spell to try. Let's see if it works." I closed my eyes and took a shaky breath, praying this spell wouldn't backfire like the fire charm had. On second thought, maybe I should have given the spell to Aunt Thelma to try, and then came back up here once the cloud was gone to break into the room.

"Hello? Earth to Jelly?" Percy waved his hand in front of my face using the nickname he had saddled me with since childhood

"Will you knock that off? I'm getting my thoughts together."

"You don't need to think. Just swish and flick and get this snow out of here."

"If it's so easy, I'd like to see you try it."

"All right then, hand over your wand." Percy motioned at me with his fingertips.

I shook my head. The day I gave a poltergeist my wand was the day I'd officially lost my mind.

I reread the spell Connie had written down for the nine hundredth time. Encanto kairos vamos. Encanto kairos vamos. Encanto kairos vamos. I said it three times in my head.

"Okay, here it goes." I exhaled a shaky breath.

Clearing my throat, I raised my arm to the cloud and proclaimed, "Encanto kairpos varmos!"

At first, it appeared as if nothing had happened. Snowflakes continued to sprinkle steadily down from the ceiling.

"Er?" Percy looked at me.

I shrugged my shoulders.

Then with a whoosh, a blast of wind rolled down the hall and blew my hair back, taking my stocking cap along with it. I turned and watched it fly down the hallway.

It was the last thing I saw.

The force of the wind scattered the snow into the air as if we were inside a giant snow globe that had just been turned upside down.

The snow began to swirl around us violently like a snow tornado. Snow and ice stung my face and stuck in my hair.

"Jelly!" Percy hollered. I knew he was in front of me, but I couldn't see him. I couldn't even see my hand in front of my face. "What have you done?"

It wasn't every day' I could freak Percy out, but today was one of them.

"I don't know!" I confessed. "I must've said the spell wrong!"

"Fix it!"

"Let me see." I held my wand in the air even

though I couldn't see anything in front of me. "Erase-O? Go-away-O?"

"Quit adding 'O' to the end of every word. Even I know that's not how spells work!"

"You're right! You're right!" I needed to think, but it was impossible to with snow and wind assaulting us from every direction.

I felt my tiger eye necklace grow warm around my neck. The swirling snow seemed to slow as time slowed. The pendant continued to heat up, reminding me that I was magic personified. Every cell of my being was enchanted. I only needed to open my mind and trust my intuition. I had all the answers I needed inside. I closed my eyes and ignored the raging storm surrounding us. My heart rate calmed, and my breathing leveled out. In my mind, a door appeared. I had no idea where it came from, but it glowed a soft blue color, calling me forward. I walked toward it without thinking and touched my hand to the knob. Like my pendant, the knob grew warm to my touch, bathing me in warmth from the tip of my nose to my toes. I twisted my wrist, and with a soft pop, the door released and swung inward. Blue light spilled out and around me. I tipped my face up and felt the power wash over me. Somewhere from deep inside, my magic was released, and suddenly my powers, the ones I hadn't even realized had been bound, were free.

I slowly opened my eyes and knew exactly what to do.

I slowly waved my wand in the air, commanding the wind to be steady, and as the snow cleared, I aimed at the cloud and said, "Encanto kairos vamos," in a calm, confident voice. I didn't second guess the spell or overthink it. My magic responded instantly, vanishing the cloud and taking the snow along with it.

I turned to Percy with a big grin on my face. He stood there with his mouth wide open.

"You did it. I can't believe you did it," he said after finding his voice.

My body tingled as I felt a new source of power run through my veins.

"I knew you had it in you," Percy beamed. "We all knew it."

It took me a minute to come down from my magical high. I had a million questions, like who had bound my powers, and how long ago did it happen? I didn't have any problems with my magic when I was a child or even a teenager. It wasn't until I came back to

Silverlake that my magic was hit or miss. It wasn't like I couldn't do anything right, but never consistently. I thought I had only needed a refresher course, but now I knew that wasn't true. My magic had been locked away. Inaccessible. Again, I wanted to understand how and why, but those questions would have to wait. I had a case to solve.

And it started with searching Paige's room.

No, wait. That wasn't right. Call it magic or intuition, but the voice in the back of my head was telling me to go to Rebecca's room first.

Percy left me on the second floor to brag about me to Eleanor. Those were his words, not mine. So, I was free to explore on my own. As far as I knew, Sheriff Reynolds hadn't searched Rebecca's room. Even better, he hadn't told us to stay out.

I'd planned on sneaking downstairs and trying my newfound powers out on Rebecca's lock, but it turned out I didn't need to sneak at all. Aunt Thelma was sitting cozy-like by the fire with Mayor Kringle. The two sat across from one another. A plate of cookies and two mugs sat on the coffee table between them. Neither one paid me any attention as I walked in front of them and behind the registration desk. I had an extra key to Rebecca's room a moment later.

Bits of their conversation floated over. It sounded like Mayor Kringle was shocked to hear about

Megan, and Aunt Thelma comforted him the best she could.

"I'm sure we'll get to the bottom of this real soon," she replied hopefully.

"I wanted to spend more time with you, but not like this," the mayor confessed.

"Me too," Aunt Thelma replied softly. I smiled to myself at the sweet exchange. My aunt had terrible luck when it came to relationships. She had spent a lifetime looking for true love, and all she had found was heartache along the way. I secretly hoped her luck was turning around.

In no time, I was standing in front of Rebecca's room. I glanced over my shoulder to the left and then to the right. Seeing the coast was clear, I swiped the plastic key in front of the sensor and waited for the light to turn green. The moment it did, I lowered the handle and released the lock, allowing the door to swing inward. Or it should have worked that way, in theory.

"What the heck?" Something on the other side of the door was preventing the door from opening all the way.

I peered in the crack and couldn't believe the mess that awaited me. Someone had thrown clothes on the floor along with all the bedding. Mixed in with the linens were the contents of Rebecca's suitcases and the empty dresser drawers. The person had yanked the wooden drawers out and discarded them haphazardly on the floor. From the looks of it, Rebecca had packed a lot of clothes and shoes.

It turned out a black high heel had been wedged under the door. Nothing that a little muscle wouldn't fix. I rammed my shoulder into the door like I had seen cops do on police shows dozens of times. Unfortunately, no one mentioned how much your shoulder hurts after it hits the door and makes it open.

"Ouch," I remarked, rubbing my shoulder.

That thought quickly faded when I took in the full scope of the mess.

"Oh. My. Wand," I said in awe. I stood at the threshold, my hands on my hips. Either Rebecca had been a complete slob, or someone was looking for something. It was the only explanation. The person had even slashed the pillows, spilling the filling out onto the carpet. The drapes appeared to be the only things untouched.

I didn't even bother to enter the room. Instead, I stepped back and allowed the door to swing shut and lock.

Doing a one-eighty, I backtracked through the lobby.

Aunt Thelma noticed me this time as I passed through. I replied with a strained smile. I knew I had to call the sheriff and tell them what I'd found, but I wasn't ready to do that yet. If Rebecca's room was tossed, did that mean Paige's had been as well?

I tried to think back to the winter scene, but it was impossible to know the state of the room underneath all that snow. But the bathroom had been a block of ice, and I still wanted to know if broken glass was mixed in.

I marched back upstairs with purpose. Connie's spell had worked well to vanquish the snow cloud. I wondered what it would do to the rest of the winter scene? There was only one way to find out.

I briefly stopped back in at the apartment on the third floor for a new hat and an extra sweater and gloves. If the spell didn't work, I wasn't going to freeze my fingers off searching Paige's room.

I jogged down the steps as quietly as possible and swiftly walked down the corridor until I faced Paige's door. The transparent film still clung to the frame, locking the storm inside.

"Magic, don't fail me now," I said to myself as I fished Paige's room key out of my pocket. Again, I waited for the light to turn green and then attempted to open the door. The door was stuck, just like Rebecca's had been, but it was because of the snow this time.

It was time to do something about that.

I tucked Paige's room key back in my pocket and withdrew my wand. Instantly, my tiger's eye felt warm and heavy around my neck, reminding me that I could handle this.

I know, I told myself.

"Encanto kairos vamos," the words rushed past my lips and sailed into the room, sucking the snow into the ether along with it.

"Ha!" I shouted before remembering I was trying to be sneaky. Still, I couldn't keep the smile off my face.

The door opened freely now. I repeated the spell two more times, watching the snow magically disappear. Connie was a genius. She just didn't know it yet.

As the snow vanished, Paige's room came into focus. It looked nothing like Rebecca's. Everything was neat. Paige had made her bed, and she zipped her suitcase up tight.

The bathroom was another story.

"Are you sure Rebecca wasn't here?"

Paige didn't look like the makeup type. In fact, I didn't think she wore much, if any, but the bathroom counter was littered with cosmetics. As the ice melted, I spotted tubes of foundation, makeup sponges, tins of lipgloss, stacks of eye shadow pallets with their miniature rectangles of shimmering powders, and round blush compacts. A makeup case, which looked like a master angler's tackle box, took up the rest of the counter. I bent closer to the counter, careful not to touch anything, and about jumped up in surprise.

"I was right," I whispered into the air. Mixed in with the powders and creams were shards of glass broken across the granite countertop. I used the tip of my wand to poke at one of the pieces. It moved freely along the countertop.

I quickly found my cell phone in my front pocket and took a picture of the scene. Then I continued to mentally catalog everything, using the tip of my wand to lift the towels on the floor and slide the tackle box, I mean makeup case, to the side. I couldn't believe the number of beauty products still inside it. I thought the majority of them were already splayed out on the countertop. I used my gloved fingers to lift the accordion-style drawers and stopped short.

I blinked once, and then twice, at the discovery.

I didn't know how much was there, but Paige had a stack of cash in the bottom of her makeup case. All hundreds, by the looks of it.

I took a deep breath.

Today was a day full of surprises.

THIRTEEN

I hadn't spoken to Vance since this morning, and I had a lot to tell him. "Hey, where you at?" I said when he answered the phone.

"Down at the station still. Sheriff Reynolds isn't buying Paige's story."

"You might not want to, either."

"What?" I could picture Vance scrunching his forehead.

"I found a lot of money in her room." I had so much to say, and I wasn't sure where to start. Adrenaline started flowing through my veins as I remembered how the afternoon had played out.

"How?"

"Let me back up. Connie gave me a spell to try on the cloud upstairs today, and it worked."

"It did?"

"I know, shocking. But there's more. So much more." I tried to keep to the relevant facts. "After I got that cleaned up, my intuition told me to check out Rebecca's room. Get this. Someone tossed it—utter destruction." I shook my head, unable to adequately describe the scene. "Then I thought I should try Connie's spell out on Paige's room, and it worked there too!" I knew I was talking fast, but I couldn't seem to slow down. "Once I got rid of all the snow and ice, it was easy to see that no one had searched Paige's room. It's neat as can be except for the bathroom. That was another story. There's makeup everywhere and this oversized case. Anyway, that's where I found the money. A whole stack of hundreds. Easily thousands of dollars." I took a deep breath and waited for Vance to reply. "You still there?"

"I'm here. Where are you now?"

"At the inn. I need to call the Sheriff and tell him about Rebecca's room. Oh, and we need to get the word out about the spell. See if we can't get rid of this snow once and for all." I wasn't sure how it would work on a grand scale, but we had to try.

"You must really want to go on vacation." I could hear the smile in Vance's voice.

"More than you know."

"I'll step out and tell the sheriff about the room and spell."

"Okay, I'm going to go give my aunt a head's up."

"After that, do you want to meet up for dinner?"

"Sure, the diner?"

"Sounds good."

"I'll call you after the sheriff leaves." I didn't want my aunt to have to deal with Sheriff Reynolds on her own.

"Okay, talk to you soon."

I hung up with Vance and went out to the lobby to break the news to my aunt.

"What's going on now?" Mayor Kringle said to me after I spoke privately with my aunt. I looked over at my aunt to see how much she wanted to relay to her friend.

"Just another piece of the puzzle," she explained. "Like I said, we'll figure this out yet."

"You did what now?" Sheriff Reynolds stood in front of me, hands on his hips, with a scowl on his face. The man was not impressed that I'd unlocked Rebecca's room.

"I opened her room. You didn't say not to. It was a regular housekeeping call." I was careful to keep my expression innocent.

"Vance said someone's tossed it?" The sheriff looked skeptical.

"Come see for yourself." I motioned with my head for the sheriff to follow me. Just then, his daughter strolled into the lobby. I continued to lead the sheriff down the hall, hoping that Amber would go away.

"What did you do now?" The woman's voice came from behind me.

I closed my eyes and counted to three before speaking. "I didn't do anything except open Rebecca's door." I demonstrated the movement then, swiping the card, waiting for the light to turn green, and pushing down the handle.

"And now your fingerprints are all over the handle," Amber rolled her eyes.

"They already were from the first time," I replied. The door swung freely open this time.

I stayed out in the hallway while Sheriff Reynolds snapped on gloves and proceeded into the chaos.

I was still standing out in the hallway when Vance appeared.

"Hey, I thought you were still at the station."

"Thought you might need some backup." Vance bent low and planted a kiss on my cheek.

"Thanks. Amber's in there." I motioned to the door with my head.

"Want to head back to the lobby?"

"I suppose. No sense standing out here. They might be a while."

No sooner were the words out of my mouth when the sheriff opened the door.

"Cataloging that mess is going to take a while."

I nodded. "For what it's worth, I didn't go in once I saw it."

"For what it's worth," Amber mocked me, "consider this your warning."

I bit my tongue. Nothing good would come out if I opened my mouth.

"Amber's right. This is now a crime scene. Make sure you stay out. Paige's room too."

"About that..." I looked over at Vance. Maybe now was a good time to retain a lawyer.

"I don't think the sheriff's been that mad at me in a long time," I said as I dunked my fries in ketchup.

"Not since you outsmarted him with that last case, anyhow."

I conceded Vance's point. "He should be happy I'm helping."

"I agree, but you and I both know that's not going to happen."

"No, I suppose not." I thought back to the past twenty-four hours and remembered I hadn't told Vance about unlocking my powers. I went on to explain the scene this afternoon and the accompanying power surge.

"Someone bound your powers?"

"That's what I think. I don't know how else to explain it."

"Who would do that?"

"Good question. I don't know. I was going to ask Aunt Thelma what she thought, but she's been occupied."

"She really likes Mayor Kringle." It was a statement and not a question.

"She does. I told her to go for it. She deserves to be happy." I shrugged. "Maybe nothing will come of it, but you never know if you don't try."

"Is that what brought us back together?" Vance asked with a glint in his eye.

"Something like that." I looked up at Vance and smiled.

Vance's expression sobered. "We only have until tomorrow to cancel our reservations and get a refund."

I frowned. I didn't want to cancel our trip, but I

didn't see how we'd have this case solved in time. But I didn't want to admit defeat. Not yet. "Mind giving it another twelve hours?"

"No, I'll let it go till the last minute. I'm still praying for a miracle."

I was glad we'd found a spell to deice the town, but that still didn't restore Mayor Parrish, Megan, and Rebecca to their former selves.

I'd debated briefly about trying Connie's spell out on Mayor Parrish, but so far, all the magic did was make the ice and snow disappear. What if it did the same to Mayor Parrish? It was too risky. I wasn't willing to play chance with someone's life. And I didn't feel right leaving for vacation when they were still being kept on ice.

It felt wrong relaxing and having fun when people's lives were hanging in the balance.

"We need to come up with a plan." Vance had finished his burger, and stood up to bus his plate. No need to add more work for his mom to do.

"I agree, but where do we start?" I said when he came back. I had too many suspects and theories churning around in my brain.

Vance repeatedly snapped his fingers while he thought. "Remember what Luke said this morning?"

I scrunched my nose while I thought. "That he made Paige go ice skating?"

"No, before that. He said someone tried to break into The Candy Cauldron."

"We assumed it was because of Rebecca and Mayor Parrish." Because why else would someone attempt a break-in last night of all nights?

"Right," Vance agreed.

"Okay, that makes sense. So, why don't we set a trap and see if they take the bait." We didn't know who was behind the attempt or exactly why, but hopefully, they were desperate enough to try again.

"We just need to find out how to make sure the person knows about it."

"And what we're going to say."

Both Vance and I thought for a minute.

"I think we need to head to The Candy Cauldron. Maybe Luke can help us out."

"Good idea. Let me go pay."

"I'm going to head to the restroom, and then I'll meet you out front."

I stood and weaved my way amongst the diners, stopping briefly for Heather to swoop in and kiss me on the cheek. "Looking lovely as ever," she said with one hand balancing a serving tray filled with shakes and fries.

"Back at you."

"My son treating you right?" Heather continued to walk away.

"Always," I replied with a smile.

Heather nodded. "He better."

I turned back around and came face to face with Michael.

"You," he bit out. Michael shot me a livid glare.

I couldn't help but look affronted. "What about me?"

"You asking my grandma about me? Snooping around in my personal life?"

I crossed my arms in front of my chest. "Why do you care? You got something to hide?"

"I don't like people sticking their noses in my personal life, that's all."

"Well, I don't like people cursing my friends."

"Rebecca wasn't anyone's friend."

"I meant Mayor Parrish," I ground out.

"It doesn't matter who you meant. The bottom line is, I had nothing to do with it." Michael continued to walk toward me. "But when you find out who did, let me know. I'd like to send them a card." Michael leered as he passed by.

I sighed in frustration. It would be great if Michael were the bad guy because I really didn't like him.

FOURTEEN

As we approached The Candy Cauldron, I spotted Stormy Evans reporting outside. The air was considerably warmer, and Stormy's attire reflected the change. She'd dropped the fur-trimmed outfit for a soft pink wool coat and cream knitted gloves. I wasn't a fan of Stormy, per se, but I did like her wardrobe.

"Does it seem warmer out to you?" Vance asked.

"I was thinking the same thing. Wonder if it's Connie's doing or something else?" Around us, you could hear the steady dripping of melting icicles as the drops hit the pavement and the water flowed down the storm drains.

I stopped walking. "I think I might have the answer to our problem." I motioned to Stormy.

"Someone must've slipped and told her where the

women were at."

"My money's on Amber during her interview this morning."

Vance nodded. "You're probably right. What's your plan?"

I turned to face Vance so that our conversation was more private. "We tell Stormy that Luke's freezer is acting up, so we're going to transfer the women to the diner. Only I'm a little worried because the security isn't as tight over there."

"It isn't as tight."

"Good, because we want the bad guy to break in, and then we can catch them."

"That might work."

"It's the only thing I can think of, and if we're lucky, Stormy will tell a million of her closest friends, and the news will spread like wildfire."

I turned at the noise coming from behind me. Luke stuck his head out of his shop's door. "Are you guys going to come in?"

"Be right there," Vance said over my shoulder. "You ready to put this plan into action?"

"Let's do it." I reached for Vance's hand and together we walked up the path to Luke's shop.

"Night, Rhonda." Luke waved to his employee as she left for the night, and he ushered us in.

Luke locked the deadbolt behind us and then

returned to work, wiping the day's worth of finger-prints off his glass candy display cases.

"What did you find out? Did you get them to release Paige?" Luke stood to his full height, white cloth in hand, and looked to Vance for the answer.

I'm the one that spoke up. "Actually, no."

"What do you mean no? Paige is innocent. You'd be a fool if you didn't realize that." Luke walked away from us, mumbling to himself. "I knew I should've stayed with her. I don't care what Sheriff Reynolds said. I should have been allowed to stay."

"Don't beat yourself up, man," Vance started to say.

"You don't understand. Paige is a good person. I know we just met, but she is one of the most genuine people I have ever known. There's just something about her. I don't want to see her get taken advantage of ever again." Luke looked torn, like he wanted to say more, but he wasn't sure how much he should reveal. "She told me some things about when she was little, and she had it rough, okay? I know what that's like. You know I only have Sally and the girls. Growing up the way we did breeds a certain type of loyalty. Hard to explain, but I understand Paige."

"I know you care about her, but some things aren't adding up. We got the winter storm to die down in her room today, and the sheriff found a stack of money with her stuff." I conveniently left out my involvement in the discovery. Luke wasn't thinking rationally, and I didn't want him to take his frustration out on me. We needed him on our side if we were going to convince Stormy his freezer was acting up.

"So? People travel with money. Not everyone uses credit cards."

"It was a few thousand dollars at least, probably more. Add that to the fact that Megan was attacked in her room means that Paige is still a suspect."

Luke ran his fingers through his hair, then paused and grabbed a fistful, tugging in frustration. "She's been set up then. Can't you guys see that?" Luke pushed off the counter and began to pace.

"You might be right. That's why we're here, and we need your help. You said someone tried to break in last night, right? We want to set them up to try again," I explained.

Luke quit walking. "Okay, I'm listening."

"Ange thinks we should tell Stormy your freezer is acting up, so we're going to move the women."

"I thought we should say that we're moving them to the diner. Then I'll add that we don't have the security over there, so hopefully, it would only be for tonight."

Luke looked uncertain. "I'm not a fan of having

them in my freezer, but I don't think we should move them."

"We're not actually going to move anyone. We're just going to pretend to," I added.

"Then we sit and wait at the diner for someone to break in, and when they do, we grab them." Vance made it sound so easy.

"I'd like to do the grabbing," Luke said with determination in his eyes.

"That's fine by me." I held my arms up in a hands-off gesture. I might have unlocked my powers, but that didn't mean I was eager to use them. I was more than happy to be backup.

"Is everyone good with the plan then?"

Both Luke and Vance agreed. "Good, because it looks like Stormy is off the air. I'm going to go out there and set the trap before they leave. Luke, do you have any truffles or anything I can take out there?"

"Coming right up." Luke spun on his heels and quickly put together two small cartons of truffles.

"Thought the cameraman might like one." Luke shrugged.

"I'm sure Cameron will appreciate it. Lock the door after me." Luke's gesture was brilliant because I actually knew Cameron. It wouldn't be so odd for me to walk up and strike up a conversation with them.

"Do they still want a nine o'clock update?"

Stormy asked Cameron. Up close, the TV personality looked tired. Her makeup was flawless, but she couldn't stifle a yawn or hide the fatigue in her eyes. "At least it's warmed up," Stormy added as she unbuttoned her coat.

"Let me check in with the producer." Cameron managed to balance the camera on his shoulder and pull out his cell phone from his back pocket. He used his thumb to click on the keyboard and shoot off a message. I waited until he was done before approaching.

"Hey, how's it going? Luke thought you might want a little pick me up. They're chocolate espresso truffles. Hope you like caffeine." I handed one of the white boxes to Cameron and then turned and gave the other one to Stormy. If it had been Rebecca, she would've shot back something about being on a diet or not eating chocolate after six o'clock or some other nonsense, but Stormy readily accepted the gift. "Thank you, I appreciate it. It's been a long day." Stormy's politeness took me back. Perhaps my earlier assessment of the woman had been too harsh, or maybe Stormy was finally being genuine. Sure, she was a professional and a TV personality, but right now, she was also a woman who was tired after standing all day working on her feet. I could relate to that.

"How long are they having you guys stay in town?" I directed my comment to Cameron.

"We don't know yet. I think the network was hoping there'd be a break in the case by now."

"That's what we were all hoping, but it looks like the only thing breaking down around here is the equipment," I grumbled.

"What do you mean?" Stormy immediately picked up the thread I dropped.

I looked behind me at the candy shop. "Luke's freezer is acting up. We're afraid it might die in the middle of the night, so we're moving the women over to the diner. Heather has a similar freezer over there. She's making room right now."

"It looks like our night of reporting isn't over yet," Stormy said with a sigh.

"Sorry, maybe I shouldn't have said anything. If you do report it, make sure to mention that it's only for tonight. Off the record? Heather doesn't have the security like Luke does, so it's not the safest location. We plan on figuring out a better solution tomorrow." Like capturing the bad guy tonight and threatening them until they unfreeze everyone.

"Don't worry, I never reveal my sources," Stormy reassured me.

"Thanks, I appreciate it."

FIFTEEN

orty-five minutes later, we were laying a black tarp out on the kitchen floor of The Candy Cauldron. The plan was for Vance and Luke to wrap me in the tarp and carry me over to the diner. We'd repeat the process two more times. Everyone who saw Vance and Luke would assume they were transporting the frozen women.

We were halfway out the back door when Sheriff Reynolds caught up to us. "What in the Sam Hill do you two think you're doing?"

"It's me, Sheriff," I whispered from inside the tarp.

"Angelica?" Vance had wrapped me up like a burrito, so I could still see and breathe out the top. The sheriff's face came into view.

I tipped my head up the best I could and looked up at him.

"Back inside, all three of you."

It took a minute for Vance and Luke to shuffle me back inside and unravel me.

"Start talking," the sheriff demanded as soon as I was free.

All three of us started talking at the same time.

"You see," I said.

"Our plan was," Vance added.

"Paige is innocent," Luke finished.

"One at a time. Jeez." Sheriff Reynolds closed his eyes in exasperation.

"Let me," I said to Vance and Luke. Luke motioned for me to be his guest. "Someone tried to break into The Candy Cauldron last night. We think it's whoever cursed the town. We're trying to set a trap at the diner to get them to try it again so we can catch them." I looked over to Vance and Luke, "That about summarizes it?"

"And Paige is innocent," Luke repeated.

"Right," I agreed for his sake.

"You think the person is foolish enough to try it again?" Sheriff Reynolds looked unsure.

"I'm hoping they're desperate enough. There's a difference." The sheriff looked like he wanted to object, but I didn't give him a chance. "I think we owe it to Mayor Parrish and the others to try. Don't you?"

The sheriff deflated like a balloon. "Give me the details."

I went on to explain the plan in its entirety, ending with, "So, you see, we need to keep a low profile."

"I know how to run an undercover operation, Ms. Nightingale," the sheriff reminded me.

"Right. So, does that mean you'll help us?" I asked.

"As much as it pains me to admit, we don't have a lot of options."

"Care if I get back in the tarp then?"

The sheriff mumbled something that sounded an awful lot like *heaven help me* and then signaled with his finger to get a move on.

"My presence should add a bit of credibility, I would think."

"Oh, most definitely," Vance said to Sheriff Reynolds as he tucked the tarp around my legs, and I held on to the top part and rolled across the floor. I held still for Luke to secure the plastic with duct tape, and on the count of three, they lifted me. Vance carried the top portion, and Luke got my legs.

"Mind getting the door, Sheriff?" It was Luke who had asked.

"Right, I'll get it."

And then we traveled through Village Square.

I wanted to ask what was going on outside. Was anyone paying attention? But I didn't dare open my mouth.

"How's it going?" I heard Vance say to a passerby as we walked.

Unfortunately, I couldn't make out the reply.

Ten minutes later, I was safely unrolled in the diner's kitchen.

Heather was more than willing to go along with the plan.

"You need me to close early?" Vance's mom looked at her watch. "We have about twenty minutes left of the night. I can turn over the sign if you want."

"No, I think we should make everything look as normal as possible. We don't want to tip the intended intruder off."

"Just go about your business," the sheriff agreed.

"Right, well, I better do my rounds, then." Heather picked up a pitcher of iced tea. "You just let me know if you need anything."

We all agreed that we would.

It turned out working undercover was really boring. After the initial excitement wore off and the hours ticked by, I found my eyelids growing heavy and my backside growing numb sitting on the diner's kitchen floor in the dark.

"You still awake?" Vance whispered to me. I had been resting my head on his shoulder.

"Barely," I mumbled.

"I think Luke is asleep." Vance motioned to the bundle curled up in the corner.

"No, I'm not," Luke muttered from under his coat. He had turned the clothing around and used it as a makeshift blanket. "Does your mom have anything to eat?" Luke poked his head up.

It sounded like a ridiculous question given where we were, but I knew what Luke meant. He wanted to know if Heather had something we could eat that didn't require using the kitchen or turning on the lights.

"Pie?" Vance threw the suggestion out there.

"Oh, I wonder if she has any banana cream?" I questioned. I loved cream pies.

"I could use a slice of apple myself," Vance said, pushing up off the wall and standing up. "Oh man, I hate that feeling. My legs are asleep." Vance winced and shifted his weight from side to side.

I leaned back against the wall and turned my head from side to side, allowing my neck to crack.

"I could go for pie," Luke said, standing up as well. "What time is it anyway?"

"Almost two." I pulled out my phone to double-check. I had spent the first couple hours of the stakeout scrolling my phone and reading every social media post and news article that interested me.

Luke copied me and also brought his phone out. "Did you see how many videos people have posted from New Year's Eve?" he said as he walked over.

"Yeah, Misty showed me a couple."

"Sally just sent me one. Look at this. Watch closely." Luke turned his phone around, and Vance and I huddled together to look at the small rectangular screen. We watched the final ten seconds of the countdown and the resulting blue flash of light. "Did you see that?" Luke asked, pointing at his phone.

"See what exactly?" I asked.

"Yeah, I'm not seeing anything new."

"It looks like a double flash. There's a bright blue one and then a smaller white one, almost like a bolt of lightning. Here, let me show you again. I'll slow it down this time."

Vance and I carefully paid attention as the footage repeated. "There, right there." Luke paused the phone at precisely the right moment.

"You're right. There is a second flash." I couldn't believe it.

"It's almost impossible to see, but I think you're right."

"What does that mean, though?" I asked.

"I'm not sure, but I think it means more than one spell is involved," Vance said.

"You're probably right. Gosh, this is just getting more and more convoluted."

"I say we bust out the pie and think about this some more," Luke offered.

I was going to say I agreed when I heard a sound outside the back door. "Shhh, do you hear that?" It could be the sheriff, seeing as he was keeping an eye on the diner from out front, but I wasn't taking any chances. "Everyone get into their places," I hissed.

We dashed around the kitchen in the dark, our sneakers squeaking on the tile floor. I grimaced, hoping our mad dash hadn't alerted the intruder.

"Freeze spell," I whispered to Vance as if he needed a reminder of what spell we were going to use. Luke's job was to block the door and prevent the intruder from escaping. The plan was simple, and that was the beauty of it.

It felt like an eternity, but it was probably only ten seconds before the back door creaked open. The figure was barely inside when I nodded to Vance and together we shouted, "Glacio!"

An electric blue light shot out from our wands and hit the target dead center.

"Oh!" The woman managed to say before she was frozen.

"Quick, get the lights!" I said to Luke.

Sheriff Reynolds came barreling through the door a moment later, almost squishing Luke between the door and the wall in the process.

"OOF!" Luke said.

"Did you get her? I saw her break in." Sheriff Reynolds turned his head from side to side.

"Oh my goodness, it's our mystery woman." It was a lady I'd been looking for off and on the last couple of days.

"You know her?" Sheriff Reynolds asked me.

"I saw her at the party. She was watching Rebecca, and then after the ball dropped, I saw her again. Something about her seemed off. I've been trying to find her and interview her ever since."

"Looks like now we're finally going to get that chance." The sheriff said, withdrawing his wand.

"Luke, don't let her make it out that door." The sheriff radioed to Deputy Jones. "We got her. Make sure to secure the perimeter. I'm thawing her now."

"Roger that," Deputy Jones confirmed

Sheriff Reynolds leveled his wand at the frozen woman. Her lips were parted in shock from when the spell hit. "Tixi," the sheriff said gruffly. The spell's effect was instantaneous, and the woman was free to move.

"What in the world is the matter with you? You don't go around freezing people." The woman's hand was on her hip and her lips were moving a mile a minute.

"Ma'am, you are under arrest for freezing this town and three of its citizens. You have the right to remain silent," Sheriff Reynolds began to say.

"I don't need the right to remain silent. What I need is a lawyer from the network. This is out of hand. I was told to be here at two in the morning for the big reveal, so here I am. You're not filming this, are you? This better not be one of those gag shows. I told the network I'm not producing those anymore, and I don't like to be the butt of anyone's joke."

"Do you know what she's talking about?" Vance murmured in my ear.

"Not a clue." I cleared my throat. "Excuse me, but could you maybe back up a step or two? We have no idea what you're talking about."

"Unless you feel you should have a lawyer present." Vance held up his hand. "I don't want to strip anyone of their rights.

"I'm not guilty of anything, I can tell you that. But I might be pressing charges against you all."

"You broke in here," the sheriff reminded her.

"I most certainly did not. The door was unlocked."

We all looked to one another.

"You didn't lock the door?" The sheriff's temper quickly rose. His face reddened. It was hard to tell if it was from anger or embarrassment.

"Er, I guess not?" I looked to the guys to help me out.

"What am I supposed to charge her with then?" he exploded. "Of all the hair brained ideas you've come up with, I can't believe I let you talk me into this!"

"Okay, hang on a second. I'm sorry, what's your name again?"

"Gloria Estrada. Executive producer for Hocus Pocus."

"The reality network?" I guessed.

"That's right."

"The network sent you here?" Vance looked unsure.

"That's what I assumed. I had to sign a nondisclosure agreement. My assistant handled it. It's all industry-standard, right down to the cash allowance and accommodations."

"And the network told you to be here at two

o'clock this morning? You didn't think there was something odd about that?" Sheriff Reynolds asked.

"You've never worked in television, have you?" the woman replied dryly.

"Can't say that I have."

"Good TV doesn't care what time it is. You go where the story is."

I turned to Vance while the sheriff and Gloria debated what constituted good television, and Luke rifled around in the fridge for something good to eat. "I don't think the network sent her here. Not to the diner, anyway."

"I don't think so either. Hang on a second." Vance looked out the window and then turned and bolted out the door without another word.

"What's going on?" The sheriff hollered, but Vance didn't slow down. He was out the door in a flash. "Vance!" I shouted after him and ran to catch up. Luke and the sheriff weren't too far behind me.

SIXTEEN

Whomever Vance had seen, he was close on their tail. I had to be careful not to slip on the remaining ice as I ran down the cobblestone streets of Village Square. The shopping district was hard to navigate on the dark and snow-packed paths.

"Slow down!" I heard Vance yell. "We need to talk!" Vance's voice echoed down the alleyway.

"Magemenos!" Came the reply in a voice I barely recognized. A bolt of lightning shot back in our direction. I was still thirty feet behind Vance, coming up quickly, when the spell hit Vance in his shoulder. He staggered backward as if he was ready to trip and fall, when his entire body transformed before me into an ice sculpture.

I skidded to a halt in front of Vance. The curse

had transformed my beautiful soulmate before my eyes. Vance's body was frozen solid, every detail of his clothing and expression perfectly preserved in ice. His eyes were wide and his mouth was open as if he was in the middle of saying something. I couldn't believe this was happening to the person I loved more than anything in the world. I felt like I was about to lose everything.

As I stood there, staring at Vance's frozen form, my emotions were all over the place. Anger, sadness, and fear all battled for dominance. I wanted to scream, cry, and unleash every spell I knew all at once. My emotions spun out of control. It was a tossup between having a complete melt-down, turning into a sobbing puddle, or lashing out in rage.

I was filled with a desperate need for action, to do something, anything, to make this right. I lifted my wand and started running, firing spells in the direction I thought the attacker might be. If the perpetrator was anywhere in front of me, they would get hit and be sorry.

"Stay with Vance!" I yelled back to Luke, who was the first to catch up with me. I had to find the person responsible and make them pay for what they had done to my husband. My love for Vance was the only thing keeping me going as I charged into the night, determined to stop the person who had taken everything from me.

"You will not get away with this!" I bit off as I ran. The shadowy figure loomed before me.

"Choiros!" A red streak flew out of my wand.

"Prasinos!" A green flash raced the red streak.

"Katapa!" A blue orb formed and shot forward into the air.

The man danced around my curses, each one just barely missing its mark. But I wasn't through. We hit the front of the Village Square and were now racing across the parking lot. I could see the figure under the streetlights, and it was for sure a man. He headed straight for Wishing Well Park, probably hoping the trees would provide cover, but he wasn't going to be that lucky.

"Eye of newt, wolfsbane, venom, you will pay and then some! I curse you to the depths of night unless you stop and make things right!" I skidded to a halt as the spell erupted from my wand. A hot pink light burst out from the tip. It was brighter than the sun. I felt the heat move up my arm and shoot out into the night, fanning out as it went. The man had nowhere to escape. The curse rolled through the park like a thundercloud, covering it entirely. When it hit him in the back, gold sparks flew out into the sky like a beacon, signaling his location to everyone.

Luke hadn't listened to me. He was hot on my heels.

"I told you to stay with Vance!"

"Deputy Jones is there."

I suppose that was just as good. Deputy Jones wouldn't leave Vance. I could trust him. I couldn't say the same for myself. I wasn't sure what I would do when I unmasked the man. But one thing was for certain, this nightmare was going to end. Right now.

My spell had rendered the man immobile, His back was to us, but we had caught up to him.

Luke couldn't help it. He busted out laughing. "What in the world did you do to him?"

"I might've gotten carried away." The man had a horse's tail, elephant ears, and one arm was considerably longer than the other. It was dangerously close to dragging on the ground.

Then I recognized who it was.

I whirled in front of the man and pointed my wand at his chest. "Cameron! Why? Because you hated Rebecca, you took out your revenge on all of us?"

Cameron didn't say a word.

"I don't think he can speak," Luke replied.

I sighed. "Fine, I'll take off the spell, but if you even think about running, I'll blast you with a curse a hundred and ten times stronger. Do I make myself clear?"

"Settle down now," Sheriff Reynolds said as he jogged up to meet us.

"I'll settle down once he turns Vance back," I shot back, unable to help myself.

"What did you do to the guy?" The sheriff asked, taking in Cameron's appearance.

"He only got what he deserved," I snapped. I could deal with a lot. But when it came to someone hurting those I loved? I had no patience.

I reluctantly undid the curse after Sheriff Reynolds assured me Cameron wouldn't get away.

"Explain yourself," were the first words out of my mouth.

"I'm sorry. I swear, I didn't want to do it. Rebecca made me."

"Rebecca's been in Luke's freezer for the last two days. She didn't make you freeze Megan. And she sure didn't make you freeze Vance." Cameron wasn't getting off that easy.

"I know, but what was I supposed to do? Megan figured it out, and Vance saw me."

"Why, though? Why did you do any of this to begin with?" I wanted to grab Cameron by his shoulders and shake some sense into him.

"It was Rebecca's idea. She wanted to go viral.

She's trying to get a prime-time gig. That's why she invited Gloria and set her up at that fancy house outside of town. I was supposed to film everything, and then when the three days were up and the winter spell wore off, transform her back. No one else was supposed to get hurt."

"Why would you ever go along with that? It was a horrible idea. You don't even like Rebecca."

"I know, but I needed the money. Do you know how hard it is to get funding for a documentary? It's impossible unless you know somebody or you're rich to begin with. Rebecca promised me ten thousand dollars. If I hadn't agreed, I'd be stuck filming the likes of her for the rest of my life. It was a risk I was willing to take. Only it went too far. I tried to find the money and call it off."

"Son, you're already in a lot of hot water. I might remind you that you have the right to remain silent. You are in the presence of a law enforcement officer."

"It's fine. You're going to find out anyway. I ransacked Rebecca's room looking for the money. Then I remembered she used to keep her cash in that case of hers, and Paige did her makeup on New Year's Eve. So, I went to Paige's room. When Megan found me there, I freaked out. It was all supposed to end tonight, but you set me up."

"What did you expect? You can't freeze people,

not to mention an entire town, and not expect to get in trouble!" I was still livid.

"Calm down, it's going to be okay." Luke placed his hand on my shoulder.

I turned away from Cameron. "I'm sorry. Seeing Vance like that, I can't handle it." And then, much to my horror, the tears started to fall, and I couldn't stop them. "What if he can't change him back? What if I've lost Vance forever? I just got him back. What if he's gone?" I couldn't stop the what-ifs rolling through my mind. The future was too painful without Vance.

"I can change him back," Cameron piped up from behind us. "That's what I was supposed to do tonight. I'll go do it right now, if that's okay?" Cameron looked over to the sheriff for permission.

"You can, but you're walking with me this time," Sheriff Reynolds instructed.

I can't explain the relief I felt seeing Vance transformed back to his former self. I'm not even embarrassed to say I threw my arms around him and created the biggest public display of affection Silver-lake had ever witnessed. I'm told we even made Sheriff Reynolds blush.

The rest of the case, with the "whos" and "hows,"

could be figured out without us. Cameron and Rebecca were under arrest, Mayor Parrish was unfrozen, and Megan had one heck of a story to write for the Yuletide Times. Even the snow around Silverlake was slowly melting as the winter curse wore off.

Later we'd find out both Mrs. Potts and Loretta were right. Rebecca had used the countdown ball to release the potion, which contained a winter storm set to last for forty-eight hours. If Paige was guilty of anything, it was neglecting to mention her sister was a weather witch. Rebecca had started her career as a meteorologist before realizing how much she loved being in front of the camera. After that, she became obsessed with becoming famous and realized she'd never get there reporting the weather. That's when Rebecca switched over to entertainment news and hoped her stunt would catapult her career. Oh, Rebecca landed on the front page, all right. Only time would tell if she'd ever live down the notoriety.

When I got home early that morning, I found Aunt Thelma curled up on the couch, wearing her bathrobe, with a box of tissues beside her.

"Aunt Thelma, what's wrong?" Maybe I had gotten used to seeing my aunt all glammed up throughout the weekend, and it was rather early, but she looked rather worn-out and downright sad.

"Oh, nothing. I'm just having a good cry, that's all."

I looked at my aunt with a sympathetic expression. "Mayor Kringle checked out, didn't he?"

"I don't know what I expected. He has a town to run, and I have the inn to manage."

"Did he say that?"

"No," Aunt Thelma sniffled and plucked another tissue out of the box to blow her nose. "He wanted me to come with him. Oh, not right away, but he asked me to think about it. I don't see what the point is. I can't do that. I don't know who I was fooling more, him or me."

"Hush, you could make it work. Weren't you telling me how much you loved the snow?"

"Well yes, but—"

"And didn't Mayor Kringle love it here, too?"

"He said Silverlake was a lovely town."

"Why can't you have both? He's not going to be mayor forever. Why not split your time between both towns? It could be the best of both worlds."

"I couldn't ask him to do that."

"Why not? I can manage the inn while you're in Mount Holly. It's not a big deal."

"He'd think it was foolish."

I gave my aunt a look to suggest otherwise.

"Think about it, won't you? It breaks my heart to see you so sad."

"I'll be fine. Now, what's on your mind?" My aunt abruptly changed the subject, signaling she was done talking about her problems. It was a tactic I'd employed dozens of times. I guess I learned from the best.

"Me? Nothing, why?"

"You sure about that? I sense you want to ask me something."

I smiled. After saying goodnight to Vance, I couldn't help but think about my powers once more. I'd planned on asking my aunt about them, but when I got home and found her on the couch looking depressed, I hesitated.

"I promise helping you will only make me feel better."

I sighed. "Here's the thing." I then went on to tell my aunt about the scene on the second floor yesterday and unlocking my powers. I finished by saying, "I was wondering if you had any idea who would do such a thing or how I could find out?" If there was a way to trace the spell, I was confident Aunt Thelma would know how.

Aunt Thelma's expression softened. "Oh, honey, no one bound your powers."

"They did, I'm sure of it."

"You didn't let me finish. What I was going to say was that no one bound your powers except you."

"Me?" I felt indignant at the accusation. "Trust me. I never bound my powers. I would remember if I did."

"No? Weren't you the one who told me there was nothing practical about magic? Weren't you the one who ditched your wand? You spent thirteen years telling yourself magic was worthless, and you didn't want anything to do with it. That was you, wasn't it?" Aunt Thelma arched her brow.

"I did do that, didn't I?"

"You see, you locked away your powers. It's only now that you've come to fully embrace who you are, that your magic is free."

I visibly swallowed. "I'm sorry. I should never have left." Tears threatened to spill out of my eyes for the second time that night.

"Hush now. You're back. You're stronger than ever. You know who you are, and you'll never forget it ever again."

I stood up and walked over to my aunt, wrapping her in a tight hug. "I love you." I kissed her on the top of her head.

A knock on the door interrupted the moment.

I cocked my head. "Who in the world could that be?"

I walked over to the door and peered out. I couldn't hide the smile on my face.

"Mayor Kringle, good to see you."

"I'm sorry about the hour, but is Thelma here? I need to speak with her."

"Yes, come on in," I held open the door for him to enter.

"Frederick?" Aunt Thelma stood and tied her peach, silk bathrobe tight around her waist. "What are you doing here?"

"I was halfway back to Mount Holly when I realized I couldn't do it. I don't want to be there without you." Frederick quickly closed the distance and held my aunt's hands in his own. "Come with me. I'm not ready to let you go."

"Oh, Frederick," my aunt wrapped her arms around his neck, and the two embraced.

I considered that my cue to head to my room. I wasn't sure what the future held, but right now, it looked bright. Very bright indeed.

The next book in the series is Bewitched Break Inn. Check out the details here: https://books2read. com/u/mgjOB7

Stephanie Damore Complete Works

Mystic Inn Mysteries
Witchy Reservations (FREE)
Eerie Check In
Spooked Solid
Untimely Departure
Midnight at Mystic Inn

· · ·

Spirited Sweets Mysteries

Bittersweet Betrayal (FREE)

Decadent Demise

Red Velvet Revenge

Sugared Suspect

Witch In Time

Better Witch Next Time (FREE)

Play for Time

Time Will Tell

Beauty Secrets Series

Makeup & Murder (FREE)

Kiss & Makeup

Eyeliner & Alibis

Pedicures & Prejudice

Beauty & Bloodshed

Charm & Deception

ABOUT THE AUTHOR

Stephanie Damore is a USA Today bestselling mystery author with a soft spot for magic and romance, too. She loves being on the beach, has a strong affinity for the color pink (especially in diamonds and champagne), and, not to brag, but chocolate and her are in a pretty serious relationship.

Her books are fun and fearless, and feature smart and sassy sleuths. If you love books with a dash of romance and twist of whodunit, you're going to love her work!

For information on new releases and fun giveaways, visit her Facebook group at https://www.facebook.com/stephdamoreauthor/

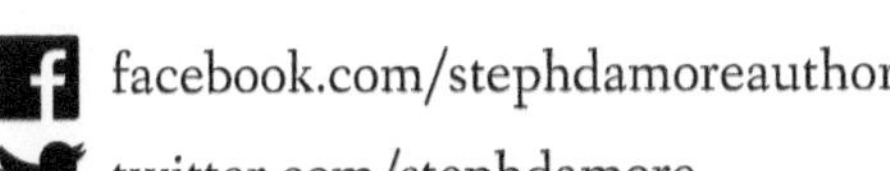

facebook.com/stephdamoreauthor

twitter.com/stephdamore

instagram.com/steph_damore_author

bookbub.com/profile/stephanie-damore